Valerian is finally safe. After years on the run, then being kidnapped, he's found a home, and if he has anything to say about it, he's never leaving it. The dragon shifters have welcomed him, and Cooper is with him, which is all he needs.

Cooper has been dead for a few years now, and he's getting used to it. Falling in love with Valerian probably wasn't a good idea, but there's nothing Cooper can do to change his feelings, and he isn't sure he wants to change them. He has his brother back, something he hadn't thought possible, and Valerian is finally safe.

What more could he want?

Valerian isn't just a psychic. His father was a mage, and so is Valerian. The mix of both abilities is interesting, mostly because he can make Cooper and other ghosts corporeal. Can he do so permanently? What will it take for him and Cooper to be together?

And what are the cockatrices and Curt up to?

Psychic of All Trades
Copyright © 2023 Catherine Lievens
ISBN: 978-1-4874-3867-8
Cover art by Angela Waters



Published by eXtasy Books Inc

Look for us online at:
www.eXtasybooks.com

# Psychic of All Trades
## It's a Psychic World 5

By

Catherine Lievens

# CHAPTER ONE

Valerian stared at the door. He wasn't a prisoner anymore, but he might as well be, since he was stuck in bed. He wanted out but wasn't sure his body would go along with the program. He should give himself more time, but his skin itched, and he needed to know for sure that he wasn't locked up in here like he'd been for so long with the cockatrices.

So even though he knew it was stupid, he swung his legs to the side of the bed and sat up.

"What are you doing?" Cooper asked, immediately there.

Valerian had to resist the urge to roll his eyes. "What does it look like I'm doing?"

"You need to stay in bed. You heard the healer."

"He said I'll be fine."

"He also said you needed to rest and that your body went through a lot."

Cooper reached for Valerian, but he didn't touch him. Valerian wondered why and whether Cooper was freaked out by the fact that when they touched, he became corporeal. That shouldn't have been the case, since Cooper was a ghost and had been dead for a while. Valerian had been surprised that it happened the first time, too. Now, he was just happy he could give this to Cooper, yet at the same time, he wished Cooper would leave him alone and do something that wasn't hovering over him, like finding his brother.

"I know better than anyone what my body went through," Valerian answered, trying not to get angry. "And I also know I'm going to go nuts if I stay here."

Cooper's expression told Valerian he knew why Valerian felt that way. That wouldn't be difficult, since he'd stuck by Valerian's side most of the time Valerian had been a prisoner. He'd found him only a week or so after Valerian had been taken, and he was still here, keeping him company.

Valerian knew how lucky he was. He'd thought things were over for him when he'd been kidnapped. The cockatrices hadn't hurt him initially, but kidnapping him meant they needed him for something and were planning to use him, and he hadn't been keen on finding out how. He still wasn't, even though he was curious.

But after he'd been taken, he'd known things would end there for him. He didn't have anyone who would look for him and worry about him—anyone who would realize he was gone.

That was when Cooper entered the scene. He'd been confused in the beginning, having wandered in the area since he'd died without anyone being able to see him. He'd wanted to know what Valerian was doing there and why he didn't leave, and Valerian had told him what he knew, which wasn't a lot. It still wasn't, which made him anxious, but he wasn't about to go back to the cockatrices and ask them what the fuck they'd been thinking.

Cooper had been his rock in the storm, the only thing that had kept him sane during the weeks of his captivity, and Valerian didn't want to lose him. He *wouldn't* lose him, especially not now that they were both safe.

Cooper sighed and sat next to Valerian on the bed. Their clothes brushed against each other, but Cooper still didn't touch Valerian. It was as if he was afraid to become corporeal. But he was a ghost—why wouldn't he want to be corporeal?

"I know why you feel that way, but is it better to stay in bed and be uncomfortable or fall down the stairs because your legs can't carry you?"

Valerian scowled. "I'm not that weak."

"You kind of are, but that's okay."

"It's not. I'm an adult man. Even though I was kept a prisoner, no one did anything to me." Valerian had worried for the first few days after he was taken, but eventually, he'd realized they wouldn't hurt him—not too much, anyway.

Cooper scowled. "I was there when that prick beat you up, remember?"

"I remember." Valerian sighed. "I know I'm not a prisoner anymore, but it scares me to be stuck here."

"I understand that, and I don't think I'm the only one. Do you want me to ask York to come and stay with you? He can keep you company."

Valerian shook his head, pressed his palms against the mattress, and pushed himself to his feet. Cooper scrambled to his feet, but Valerian wasn't going to wait for him. He put a foot forward, turned to grin at Cooper, then took another step.

His legs buckled.

He felt himself fall and tried to reach for the bed, but he was too far. He knew this would hurt, so he steeled himself. He never hit the floor. Strong arms wrapped around him from behind and hauled him up, and he found himself pressed against Cooper's chest.

A very corporeal Cooper.

Even though Valerian was angry, he allowed himself to lean against Cooper. Cooper had his back, but then, he always did. They'd become close during Valerian's captivity, and Valerian never wanted to lose him.

"I understand why you need to get out of this room," Cooper murmured as he guided Valerian back toward the bed. "But it's not a good idea for you to try to walk. You're still too weak."

"It doesn't make sense."

"Why doesn't it? Curt hit and starved you. What did you

expect? To rebound from that without worry? You need more food and rest, and I'll make sure you get it."

Even though Valerian was angry, it wasn't at Cooper. He chuckled at Cooper's words and turned to look at his friend. "That sounded like a threat."

Cooper helped him get back under the sheets. "It was. Don't you dare get up from the bed again."

"What if I have to use the toilet?"

"Then you call me, and I'll help you."

There was no way Valerian was doing that. He'd rather call out for anyone else to help him or even get to the bathroom by scooting around on his ass than ask Cooper to see him like that. He realized it was ridiculous, because Cooper had already seen him in worse situations, but things were different now that they were out of that hell.

Valerian just wasn't sure how different.

He hadn't expected to ever be free, and now, he wasn't quite sure what to do. Rest and get better, of course, but what would happen after that? The dragons hadn't talked to him yet, but he expected them to eventually. They hadn't rescued him out of the goodness of their hearts, or at least he didn't think so. They probably wanted something from him, and while at least they weren't beating and starving him, he wasn't sure he should give it to them. He didn't know them well enough to be able to make a decision.

He twisted to his side and buried his face against his pillow. He'd hated his life before and wasn't sure he liked it now. He didn't enjoy feeling like he needed someone to keep an eye on him twenty-four-seven, even if that someone was Cooper.

"How about I open the door?" Cooper asked. "That way, you can see the people walking in the hallway outside the bedroom."

"Fine." That would be better than staring at the ceiling or

out the window. The clan seemed to be in a lovely place, but Valerian had enough of staring at trees.

Cooper looked from Valerian to the door.

Valerian realized what the problem was and groaned. "Never mind," he said.

"Okay, so I can't open the door, but I can go look for someone to keep you company."

"You're enough."

Cooper patted Valerian's hand. "I might have been once, but now you know all my secrets. I have nothing new to tell you, so I understand why you're bored."

Valerian glared at him. "I'm not bored of you." That would never happen, but Valerian felt vulnerable enough as it was. He couldn't admit that.

"Not of me, but of the situation you're in. Let me do this for you, Valerian."

"You're going to do it even if I say no," Valerian pointed out because that was how things usually went between them.

Cooper grinned, and like that, he was even more handsome.

But that wasn't something Valerian could think about. Cooper was dead, while Valerian was very much alive. No matter how big his crush on his friend was, he couldn't afford for it to become bigger, or worse, for it to turn into love. Cooper was never coming back. Valerian could die, but he wasn't about to unalive himself, and if anyone tried to hurt him, he'd fight back. He wasn't ready for death, even though he was a psychic and knew better than a lot of people what could happen to him once he died.

But he was very much alive, and hopefully, he'd stay that way for a long time.

Why didn't knowing that make him happy?

Cooper hovered over Valerian for a moment. He wanted to do so much more for him, but he was only one man, and one dead man at that. He wished he could give Valerian the world, but he had to be content with giving him company. There was nothing else he could do, being a ghost.

Valerian finally rested against his pillows, even though he still had a stubborn expression.

"Fine. Find me someone to talk to. But I'm not saying you're not good enough for that. You're perfectly fine to talk to as far as I'm concerned."

Cooper smiled. "You're perfectly fine to talk to, too."

Valerian rolled his eyes. "But we already know everything there is to know about the other. I get it. You don't have to stay with me here if you want to do other things. I know your brother is out there, and you've been looking for him for so long. You should spend time with him."

Cooper desperately wanted to. As soon as he'd realized what had happened to him after the car accident, he'd tried looking for his brother. He'd needed to find York and reassure him that even though he was dead, it didn't mean they would be separated. It had been only the two of them after their parents had died, and Cooper hadn't wanted to leave York alone.

But he had. He'd been dead and hadn't known how to get to York. So instead, he'd drifted off. He'd died close to cockatrice territory, and eventually, he'd found his way there. It had taken him some time to digest the fact that no one could see him, and just when he thought he had, Valerian had appeared.

Cooper had known about psychics, since his brother was one, but he hadn't expected to find one a prisoner in cockatrice territory. He'd wanted to help Valerian, but in the beginning, he'd never been corporeal, not even when Valerian tried to touch him. Besides, Valerian hadn't tried to do that initially.

They'd been wary of each other, even though they needed one another. Valerian had needed company, and Cooper had been lost and more than happy to provide him with that. It had made him less lonely, and the same had gone for Valerian.

But things were different now. They weren't in cockatrice territory anymore, and Valerian wasn't alone. He could have company if he wanted it, and it was clear he did. He'd been alone for a long time, and Cooper wasn't enough anymore. It was odd to think that, but not a problem. Cooper wanted to give Valerian everything he'd ever wanted in life. Even more, he wanted Valerian to be happy, because he hadn't had enough of that.

So he left Valerian in bed and headed to find someone to keep him company.

He hated that he wasn't enough anymore, but he and Valerian had been each other's everything for too long. They hadn't had a choice while Valerian was a prisoner, but he wasn't anymore, and it was time for him to start living again. Cooper wanted him to, especially because *he'd* never start living again.

He wasn't jealous. He'd known he'd feel this way as soon as he'd woken up and realized he was dead. He'd just wanted to get his brother back, and now, he had. There was nothing more he could want from the afterlife.

Or rather, there was, but it was better not to think about it. Valerian was alive, and Cooper was dead. Nothing would ever change that, or at least, nothing Cooper could accept. He didn't want Valerian to die. He didn't want anyone to die. He was happy as long as he and Valerian could spend time together. He didn't know how he'd react when Valerian met someone, but his crush wouldn't be enough for Valerian to stop living. Cooper wouldn't allow it to.

He left the bedroom, wondering where to go. He needed to do more for Valerian, especially considering the nightmares and everything else. His body was still weak because of what the cockatrices had done to him, but he was stubborn and wouldn't give himself time to recuperate. Cooper couldn't force him to, but it looked like Valerian's body would. He had to stay in bed at least until he was strong enough to get out of it, something he wasn't ready to accept.

Cooper understood the situation wasn't easy. There was nothing he could do about the nightmares, unfortunately, but he could find someone to distract Valerian for an hour or two so he wouldn't dwell on the nightmares and on how weak he felt.

The nightmares occurred because of what had happened with the cockatrices, but Cooper suspected there was more. He and Valerian had talked about Valerian's life before, but he'd never given Cooper many details, even after he'd realized he could trust him. Valerian didn't like to talk about it, and Cooper understood, so he'd never pushed. Besides, the situation with Curt and the cockatrices easily explained the nightmares.

If Cooper ever saw Curt, he'd make sure he knew how Cooper felt about what he'd done. Of course, Curt wouldn't be able to see Cooper since he was a ghost, but Cooper would find a way.

Once he reached the entrance, Cooper hesitated. He felt uneasy walking around the house when only a few people who lived there could see him. It was almost as if he was invading other people's private space, and he supposed he was. The alpha had agreed that he could live here, even though he couldn't see him, and Cooper was grateful for that. It meant he didn't have to worry about any of the psychics in the house noticing him and freaking out.

Cooper drifted through the house for a bit, trying to find one of the psychics. He felt like he didn't belong, and he didn't. He was dead, which meant his place wasn't amongst the living.

But he wasn't going anywhere.

Eventually, he found one of Victor's brothers in the living room. The man was looking at his phone and poking at it, with the tip of his tongue peeking out at the corner of his lips. Cooper cleared his throat, getting the man's attention.

He looked up and grinned at Cooper. "Hey."

It was still odd to think that people could see him. Until recently, it had only been Valerian and Curt's girlfriend—whom Cooper had avoided like the plague—and Cooper was still trying to make sense of all of this. He didn't just have Valerian and York anymore. He had a bunch of other psychics who could see him and made him feel like he was almost part of a family.

"Am I bothering you?" he asked.

Victor's brother shook his head. He was still looking at Cooper, and Cooper felt a bit uncomfortable. He shuffled his feet, then looked at the door, wondering if this had been a bad idea.

"You can't remember my name, can you?"

Cooper couldn't, but at the moment, that was the least of his problems. Still, he wasn't about to pour out his heart to this guy he barely knew, so he shrugged. "I'm sorry."

"Don't be. Everything's been a mess recently, and with so many people moving into this house, I'm having a hard time remembering everyone's name, too." He gave a little wave. "I'm Roslin."

"Cooper."

Roslin chuckled. "I know. Now, what can I do for you?"

"I was wondering if you or someone else could spend some time with Valerian. He's been climbing the walls and feels like a prisoner again, and he's even tried to get up and leave the room."

Roslin grimaced. "That doesn't sound good."

"Because it's not. He needs to stay in bed and rest, but it's not easy to convince him of that when he feels trapped."

"I'd be happy to visit with him and talk to him, but maybe we can think of something better. How about we ask the healer if Valerian can leave the bedroom?"

Cooper frowned. "He's too weak. He can't walk."

"He doesn't have to walk. There are plenty of strong dragons in this house. Surely we can find one of them to carry Valerian to the living room or the kitchen."

"We don't want to be a bother."

"Neither of you is. I don't know much of your history, so I understand it might feel like a lot to you, but you're part of the family now."

"I don't see how."

Roslin waved Cooper's words away. "It's convoluted, but the how doesn't matter. The only thing that does is that you *are* family, as is Valerian, and I'll be more than happy to invade his bedroom and keep him company."

For the first time in a while, Cooper found himself relaxing. He wasn't sure he entirely believed Roslin, but maybe he didn't have to. Maybe he just had to remember that he'd found a place where he belonged.

# Chapter Two

Valerian groaned at the sound of someone knocking on his bedroom door. A few days ago, he and Cooper had bickered because Valerian had tried getting up. Cooper had brought him one of the psychics who lived in the house, Roslin, and that had seemed to be the beginning of the end of peace for Valerian. For an hour, he'd been happy to have someone to talk to. The problem was that his bedroom seemed to have acquired a revolving door since then. Someone was always knocking and asking if he needed company, and he never had the heart to tell them he was fine on his own. He wasn't entirely sure that was the truth.

*Was* he fine on his own? Or was that something he'd told himself when he was with the cockatrices?

He realized he'd been lucky he'd lasted for as long as he had. After Cooper had found him, it had been easier to resist the things Curt had come up with. Valerian would never have said yes to working with Curt, but sometimes it hadn't been easy to hold strong. He'd been alone and terrified, and a lot of the time in pain. Curt knew what he was doing when it came to that kind of torture, and Valerian knew himself well enough to be aware of the fact that eventually, he'd have caved and said yes.

But he wouldn't have to, because he wasn't with Curt anymore. He was with the dragons, who'd given him a home and seemed intent on becoming his family. It wasn't just the psychics who had started to visit him. They'd dragged along their dragon shifter boyfriends and partners, and after the other dragons had realized that Valerian was fine with having them in his bedroom, they'd started coming around, too. Valerian had gone from being alone most of the time to rarely being on his own, and it was overwhelming. He'd wanted to take advantage of the fact that his bedroom was blissfully quiet right now, but it looked like he wouldn't have that opportunity.

"Come in," he called out.

The door opened, and a head poked through. Valerian recognized Elijah, the dragon alpha. He tried to get to his feet, but Elijah quickly strode toward him and raised his hand.

"Stay in bed," he said.

Valerian nodded and dug his fingers into the sheets that covered his lower body. He felt stronger today, but the last time he'd tried getting up on his own, he'd almost fallen face-first in the toilet. He was proud that he'd managed to get to the bathroom, but he'd needed Leo to rescue him, which he hadn't liked.

"How are you doing?" Elijah asked as he pulled one of the chairs that had been brought in for Valerian's visitors closer to the bed.

Valerian hesitated. Should he tell the alpha that everything was all right, or should he be honest? He didn't know Elijah well enough to be sure of how the alpha would react.

Elijah chuckled and leaned forward in his chair. "You can be honest. I've heard a few things that tell me you're not entirely happy with your stay here."

Valerian huffed. "Have people been talking behind my back?"

"Not exactly. Every person who came to talk to me about you did so because they were worried. They wanted to know what they could do to help you."

Valerian looked at his lap. He'd been alone most of his life, and even when he hadn't been, he couldn't count on more than one or two people, if even that. He wasn't used to having such a big group of people worry about him and wanting to make sure he was all right, and he didn't know what to do about it or even if there was anything he should do. He'd need to thank all of them, but how? Words didn't feel like enough.

Nothing did.

"Why don't you think about it?" Elijah offered. "You're part of the clan now, and if there's anything I can do to make you happy and make it easier for you to recuperate, I want to do so."

"Why?" Valerian asked. He could hear the desperation in his voice, but he wasn't sure Elijah could. He just needed to know why these people were doing all of this for him. They didn't know him. He wasn't one of them, yet they'd been more welcoming than anyone else ever had been in Valerian's life.

Elijah's smile was gentle and understanding. "I just said why. You and Cooper are part of our family, although I'm not quite sure how to deal with that. We've never had a ghost clan member."

Valerian snorted. "That's not true. There's Kenneth."

Elijah rolled his eyes. "Yes, I suppose there is. He seems content to spend time with his family, though. He's easy to take care of, certainly easier than the living members of my clan. They're not who I'm worried about, though. You are, and I'd like to know if there's anything I can do for you."

Valerian wasn't an idiot. He didn't doubt that Elijah was worried about him, but he was also worried about what the cockatrices had wanted from him. There had to be a reason they'd taken Valerian, and while Curt had tried to convince Valerian to help him, he hadn't explained what that meant. Valerian supposed he would have found out if he'd said yes, but he hadn't, and he didn't plan to.

So where did that leave him?

He could leave the clan behind and go back to his lonely

life. He was used to it, or at least he had been before he was taken. It would be hard to be on his own again, but he'd survive. He had before, and he was still strong.

But he didn't *want* to have to go through that again. He might not have expected the clan and everything that came with it, but he wanted to stay. He didn't know if it was a foolish decision or the best one he could make, but here, as he looked at Elijah, he knew what to do.

If he wanted to stay, he needed to be honest. He wanted Elijah to know everything there was to know about him before deciding to welcome him into his clan.

"My father was a mage," Valerian said. He looked down at his hands again, not wanting to look at Elijah as he explained his past. "He was part of a coven, and they kept to themselves like most covens do. They worked jobs for humans, but when they weren't working, they stuck to their house. My father met my mother while he was on a job his clan had sent him on, and they fell in love. But she was a psychic and not a coven member, which meant she wasn't welcome there. My father decided to leave the clan when they told him that, and for a few years, they were happy." Or at least, Valerian liked to think they had been. "Then they had me, and the coven was outraged. From their point of view, mages and psychics shouldn't mix."

"Why?" Elijah asked softly.

"Because it gives the child that is born from the union too much power. I'm both a mage and a psychic, and it's not something a lot of people can say. When I was born, the coven decided to come after us. We were on the run for most of my life, and it was normal for me. It's the only way I ever knew my family."

Valerian swallowed. It was always hard to think about this, let alone talk about it.

"Take your time," Elijah murmured.

There was no rush in his voice, nothing telling Valerian he was impatient. Valerian still didn't know if he could trust the dragons and Elijah, but he wanted to. Something told him they would be good for him, and he hoped it was true.

He needed it to be.

"I was fifteen when the coven caught up with us. They demanded my parents hand me over. They were going to kill me, but they wouldn't have hurt them. I was the problem, not them, even though they dared create someone like me. They told the coven to fuck off." Valerian chuckled darkly. "They fought, and the coven won. My mother made sure I knew how to escape if something like that happened, and I did exactly that. I had to leave them behind, and by the time I was able to go back, there was nothing left. The coven had killed both of them."

Tears pricked Valerian's eyes, and one rolled down. He reached up to dry his cheek, but someone else's hand got there before he could. He looked up at Cooper, and his heart expanded.

Cooper hadn't meant to spy on Valerian as he talked about his family, but he was glad he had. Valerian needed him more than ever, and he might not have known if he hadn't been listening. Besides, Valerian had known he was there. He could see him.

Cooper dried the tear on Valerian's cheek, then sat next to him on the bed. Valerian snuggled against him, and while Elijah couldn't see Cooper, he could see that Valerian was leaning against an invisible chest. It had to be odd, but he didn't react.

"I've been on my own since then," Valerian continued. "I drifted from town to town, making a few friends here and there, but I was too afraid to settle anywhere. The coven hasn't found me again, but I wouldn't put it past them to still be looking for me."

"How long have you been on the run?" Elijah asked.

"Seven years. I'd just arrived in town when Curt found me. I don't know how he found out I have these powers, but they're why he took me." Valerian sucked in a breath and finally looked up at the alpha. "So, you see, it's not just about Curt and the cockatrices. You might also have trouble with the coven if they ever find out where I am, and I can't promise they won't attack the clan to get to me."

Elijah leaned back in the chair and linked his fingers together over his stomach. He stared at Valerian for a moment, and while Valerian wanted to wiggle in his seat because the alpha's gaze felt heavy, he stayed as still as possible. That was easier with Cooper next to him, protecting and supporting him.

"I don't care about the coven or even about Curt and the cockatrices," Elijah eventually said. "I only care about you, and we'll deal with whatever comes next when it happens. You're family, Valerian."

"Everyone keeps saying that," Valerian grumbled.

"That's because it's true."

And it was. Cooper hadn't realized it, but when he'd found York, he'd found the dragon clan. York had fallen in love with one of the dragons here, and through Cooper being his brother and caring about Valerian, it meant Valerian was one of them, too. Cooper was happy to be able to give him at least that, and while it wasn't much, it was better than nothing.

"So the reason I'm here is that I wanted to ask you officially if you want to stay with us. You can be a clan member without living here, and you can live here without being a clan member, but I'd like for you to do both." Elijah paused and looked at Cooper. "This goes for both of you, of course."

Cooper was startled to be included, although maybe he

shouldn't be. Elijah knew he was here, and from the way he behaved, he cared about Cooper as much as he did about Valerian. It didn't matter to him that Cooper was dead. He was here, and he was York's brother, and *that* was what mattered.

But Cooper had a few questions. "Can you tell Elijah what I'm asking?" he asked Valerian.

Valerian nodded and gestured at Cooper to talk, so he did.

"I'd like to know what being a clan member entails for both of us, and I want to be sure that the clan will protect you against the cockatrices and your coven if they find you."

Valerian repeated Cooper's question so Elijah could hear it, and Cooper waited for the alpha to come up with an answer.

"We'll protect Valerian and you against anything that comes your way, be that the cockatrices or the coven. As for what being a clan member entails, it's easy. You're part of a group, a family, and that comes with certain rules, like not going into each other's private space without asking. It'll take you some time to get used to, but I doubt it'll be a problem. I also expect the two of you to work for the safety of the clan as much as you can. I understand that Valerian needs rest and not to use his magic right now, and I'm fine with that. We're on lockdown, and we have a bunch of psychics and a mage, so we can hold down the fort. The cockatrices haven't attacked, and I doubt they will, but eventually, something is going to break. I need everyone to be ready to defend the clan when that happens, and that includes the two of you."

Cooper and Valerian looked at each other. Cooper had no problem with any of that. It made sense that Elijah would want every clan member to participate in the protection of the clan, and Cooper wanted all of this for Valerian. He'd been alone for too long. Cooper wasn't going anywhere and had no intention of moving on, but he wanted Valerian to have more than him in his life.

But he wouldn't influence Valerian's decision. He knew what he wanted and wished for, but he wasn't the only one involved.

Elijah seemed to realize he wouldn't get an answer today because he got to his feet. For a second, Valerian looked panicked, but Elijah quickly put his fears to bed.

"Think about it," he said with a smile. "Talk things through with Cooper or anyone else you feel comfortable with. Maybe you could talk to York, since he hasn't been a clan member for long and knows how you might feel. I'll be here whenever you have an answer, and I'll be happy for you either way. We'll protect you, even if you decide not to become a clan member."

"Because I'm family," Valerian said. He sounded like he didn't believe it.

Elijah squeezed his shoulder. "Exactly. After what you told me about your parents and your life, I understand why it's hard for you to wrap your mind around all of this and to understand it. That's why I'm giving you more time. I want you to say yes, but I want you to do it knowing what you're saying yes to." He straightened. "And of course, you're welcome to leave your room and wander the house, although I'd check with our healer first. He won't take it well if he finds you in the hallway and he hasn't given you the okay to do so."

That brought a true smile to Valerian's lips, and Cooper found himself smiling, too.

Dying was the worst thing that had ever happened to him. He'd been drifting since then, and he'd been happy when things had improved after meeting Valerian. It had been horrible to watch Valerian be hurt, but they'd been there for each other, and it had given Cooper purpose. He didn't have to protect Valerian anymore because there were a bunch of people willing to do it for him and who would be better at it, but that didn't mean he wanted to be away from Valerian. It was just good to know they weren't alone anymore.

Elijah left the room, and Cooper started to rise, but Valerian grabbed his hand and pulled him back down. "You want to stay," he said.

Cooper didn't see a reason to lie. "I do. My brother is here, and I think you'll be safe with the dragons. Now that I know that the cockatrices and Curt aren't the only ones after you, I think it's important."

Valerian sighed. "I guess it is. I didn't want you to worry about the coven."

"Is that why you never told me about them?"

"Because of that and because I didn't think there was a reason to. I didn't expect to make it out of cockatrice territory alive."

Cooper couldn't imagine a life without Valerian. He didn't want to try, and as he wrapped his arms around Valerian and held him close, he knew he'd do anything to protect the man snuggling against him. Clearly, it was too late for him to be careful about that crush. His feelings had moved right past affection and straight into love, which would probably become a problem.

But not right now. Right now, Valerian was safe and in Cooper's arms, and that was all that mattered.


Valerian was relieved. If Cooper had said he didn't want to stay, Valerian would have left with him, but he was glad he wouldn't have to. He didn't think he'd do well away from the clan, even though he'd been alone most of his life.

Maybe that was why he wouldn't do well away from the clan. He was tired. He'd been running from the coven since he was a baby, and over the past seven years, he'd had to learn to survive on his own. His parents hadn't been there to shield him anymore or to help him and comfort him, and all of that had led to him getting captured. He had no doubt that it would happen again if he was on his own, and he wouldn't be as lucky twice. He'd survived this time. What were the odds that he would do so again?

He was glad that he wouldn't have to find out. As far as he was concerned, the clan was his home, especially with Cooper staying with him. Knowing they weren't going anywhere helped him relax, and he allowed Cooper to take more of his weight. It was odd to think that if anyone were to peek into the bedroom, they'd see Valerian snuggling on his own, but he didn't care. Everyone in the house knew he was a psychic and that there was something quirky about him that meant that Cooper could become corporeal. They'd know Cooper was there.

Or at least, Valerian hoped so, because if they didn't, they'd probably run away screaming.

"So we're staying," Cooper said.

"I guess we are. Can you imagine? We'll be living with a dragon clan."

"As long as it's better than living with the cockatrices, I don't have a problem with it."

Valerian snorted. "I don't think it's going to be hard for the people here to be nicer than the cockatrices. They've already been."

Valerian was afraid to hope he'd finally found a home, but he was done with fear. It was time for him to admit that while he'd been doing all right on his own, everything would be better with a family.

He'd missed it. He couldn't remember a life in which he and his parents didn't have to run, but even when they had to move every few months, they'd still been together. Valerian had been a typical teenager, annoyed and snarky, but his parents had never hidden the reason they were running, so he'd known why they were doing everything they did. They'd been a team, and he'd lost part of himself when they died. He'd never recover that, but maybe he didn't have to. Maybe he could give another part of himself to the clan.

"You should find Elijah and tell him we're staying," Cooper said.

Valerian pushed away from him and turned to look at him. "You're telling me to leave my bed?"

"You're doing better."

"Better, but not well. The healer is going to kick my ass if he finds me wandering around the house."

"Then maybe you should use the phone they gave you to text Elijah."

Valerian blinked. "I'd forgotten about it."

"I know. I'm pretty sure it's in the nightstand drawer."

Valerian wasn't used to having a phone. He didn't usually carry one, both because it was expensive and because he knew it could be used to trace him, but Elijah had reassured him that this one was in the clan's name, so no one would be able to identify the user. Valerian was terrified to bring the coven to the clan, especially with the cockatrices still a problem, but he couldn't live the rest of his life in fear, especially now that he did have a life.

Or that he would have one as soon as he healed, anyway.

He rolled away from Cooper and opened the nightstand drawer. He'd only been here a short amount of time, yet he'd already managed to fill the drawer with junk. He dug around until he found the phone, grinning in satisfaction as he rolled back against Cooper. Cooper welcomed him, but then he always did.

Valerian didn't know if it was because Cooper enjoyed being corporeal or because he just wanted to be close to him, and he was afraid to ask. He hoped for the latter, but he wasn't an idiot. Cooper had died extremely young. He'd be twenty-two forever, and he'd clearly decided not to move on.

Whether that was because of his brother or for other reasons, Valerian didn't know, although he was pretty sure York was a big reason for the decision. Either way, it couldn't be easy for Cooper to see so many people around him, to know that his brother was close by, and not to be able to touch him. As soon as Valerian was stronger, he'd help with that, but for now, Valerian was the only person Cooper could touch, and if that was of some comfort to him, Valerian wanted to give him that.

He turned on the phone as he snuggled back against Cooper. He could feel Cooper's fingers in his hair. It was almost enough to make him purr. He would have if he'd been a shifter, but as it was, he could only sigh in pleasure.

There were already several numbers saved on the phone, including Elijah's. Valerian felt clumsy as he opened the messaging app and quickly texted the alpha, accepting his offer.

"He hasn't asked about my powers," Valerian said out loud.

"Well, he knows you're both a mage and a psychic."

"Yeah, but he doesn't know what I can do."

"I don't think anyone does. What can you do?"

"I'm not sure." Valerian really wasn't. His parents had been teaching him before they died, but over the past seven years, he'd been on the run on his own. He hadn't had the time or opportunity to learn much, so he had no idea of how powerful he was. "I can make you corporeal," he offered.

Cooper chuckled. "I suppose that's one power. Clearly, you can see ghosts like any other psychic, but there's more to you. That has to be the mage side."

"That has to be the case, but I have no idea how to deal with it. It's not like I can ask my dad."

Cooper's arms tightened around Valerian. "I'm sorry about your parents."

"I am, too, but it's been a long time, and there's nothing I

can do to bring them back, and I can't afford to continue looking back and thinking about the past."

"What should you think about, then?"

"The future." The future Valerian had with the dragons
and, hopefully, with Cooper. Valerian didn't know if his heart
would end up broken or if they could find a way to make this
work, but he was eager to find out.

He'd always been stubborn. He knew what he wanted and
was ready to do what he needed to get it. Right now, what he
wanted was Cooper. He didn't know how he'd get him yet,
but he'd come up with something.

He always did.


Cooper had missed human contact fiercely, and Valerian
filled that need. He was the only one who could.

Cooper wished he could hug his brother, but so far, he
hadn't asked Valerian to help with that. He wasn't planning
to ask until Valerian was stronger, and until then, he didn't
think Valerian had a problem providing him with the human
touch he needed.

He shouldn't feel that way. He was a ghost, and he'd been
dead for a while. He wasn't sure how long, because being
dead meant he didn't have to keep count of the days and
weeks that passed, so he didn't. He was pretty sure that right
after his death, he'd been confused and had drifted for a
while, which didn't help. He could tell from the way York
stared at him every time they saw each other that his brother
had missed him, though, and Cooper never wanted York to
be without him.

The fact that he was a ghost was terrifying. It meant he'd
have to watch his brother grow old and eventually die. Maybe
when that happened, Cooper would finally feel ready to
move on. He certainly wouldn't be staying back if York and

Valerian didn't.

But there was no need to think about that now. Both of them were young and had their whole lives in front of them. They'd live them, grow old, and Cooper would tease them about wrinkles and white hair. And when their time came, he'd be there, waiting for them.

He blinked, wondering if ghosts could cry. His eyes prickled, but when he discreetly touched his cheek, he couldn't feel any moisture there. It didn't matter. He didn't want to cry, if anything so that he wouldn't worry Valerian.

He cleared his throat. "Do you want me to go find one of the psychics so they can keep you company? I'm sure my brother would be happy to spend time with you."

Valerian had been playing around on the phone, but he dropped it to the bed and cuddled deeper against Cooper. "I'm fine like this. Unless you have something better to do than to snuggle with me?"

Valerian and Cooper always touched a lot. They'd started when Valerian was still a prisoner, and it had been a comfort for both of them. Cooper had needed human touch, and Valerian had needed comfort and someone to tell him everything would be all right. They'd even been planning to try to use the fact that Cooper could become corporeal to get Valerian out of cockatrice territory, but they hadn't had the opportunity to make it happen because they'd been rescued before they could.

They didn't have a reason to touch as much as they did now, but since Valerian didn't seem to have a problem with it, Cooper wasn't about to push him away. He'd never be able to do that, not to Valerian.

Not to the man he was falling in love with.

If Cooper had still been alive, his heart would be racing. He'd repeatedly told himself not to develop feelings for Valerian, because it could only end in a disaster, but he didn't see how he could avoid it. Valerian was everything Cooper could ever want from a partner. He was brave and strong, sweet and gentle. He offered comfort when Cooper needed it, and he was ready to accept comfort when he was the one in need. They'd been there for each other in hard times and were still there for each other in better times.

But Cooper was dead. There was no denying that, even though Valerian could touch him and snuggle against him. That meant they couldn't be together.

Or at least, Cooper didn't think they could.

He supposed that since touching Valerian made him corporeal, they could be together in some ways, but Cooper would never be fully a part of Valerian's life. Too many people in the clan couldn't see him, and he could only imagine how awkward things would be. Besides, thinking about being with Valerian made Cooper feel like he was taking something from him. Valerian would be better off with someone still alive who could give him everything he needed.

Cooper didn't think he was that someone. None of this was fair, but he couldn't deny it.

He'd been twenty-two when he died. He'd never been in love, or at the very least he'd never felt what he felt for Valerian for anyone. He didn't want to give it up, but he couldn't think about himself. *Valerian* should be his focus, especially in this situation. He didn't know if Valerian felt the same, but he wouldn't ask. He wasn't strong enough to take a step back but wouldn't push forward. If Valerian did, they'd deal with it together.

And in the meantime, Cooper would be here for Valerian, providing him everything he could, be that cuddles, a shoulder to cry on, or love.

# CHAPTER THREE

Valerian hobbled down the hallway, telling himself he could do it. He still felt weak, but he was walking on his own, and he was proud of that.

He snorted and pressed a hand against the wall. Why was he proud of himself for walking? He was an adult. Of course he could walk. It shouldn't feel like an accomplishment, no matter what the dragon healer kept telling him. Valerian was very much aware of the fact that he'd been starved and beaten, kept prisoner in a small room, and that Curt's girlfriend had used her magic against him. She was both a mage and a psychic, and Valerian had been surprised to see her the first time. He'd expected her to feel a sense of kinship with him, but he couldn't have been more wrong. She'd been right there with Curt, hurting Valerian, and he hated her for that. He hadn't even been able to rely on Cooper when she was there because she would have seen him, and Valerian had been terrified that she'd somehow take him away. She would have found a way to make that happen. She was just as evil as Curt.

But Valerian didn't want to think about them anymore. He wanted to focus on the end of the hallway and get there, so that was what he did.

"It's good to see you out of the bedroom," a voice said behind him.

He turned to glare at the person, only to realize it was a ghost. He recognized Kenneth. He'd seen him with Cooper a few times, and it was good to know that Cooper wasn't the only ghost around the house. Kenneth had taken Cooper under his wing as the resident ghost, and they'd been spending more time together now that Valerian was feeling better. He and Kenneth had talked a few times, but they weren't friends or anything like that.

Maybe that could change now.

Valerian straightened and leaned against the wall. "Good morning to you, too."

Kenneth grinned. "Good morning. You're sure you have the authorization to be out here walking around?"

"I am. I'm not about to get my ass kicked, thank you very much."

Kenneth's laugh boomed. "I wouldn't want that to happen, either. How are you feeling, though? You're a bit pale."

"That would be because I'm tired."

Kenneth looked up and down the hallway. "Are you *sure* you're supposed to be alone? What's going to happen if you fall and hurt yourself?"

"I'm just walking. I'm not going to get hurt."

Kenneth didn't look convinced. Valerian was getting used to people butting into his life, although it wasn't always easy. Sometimes he had to resist the urge to snap and tell the person who worried about him to fuck off. He realized they were pushing because they cared, even though part of him didn't understand why.

But he didn't have to understand why these people cared about him. He just had to accept that they did and deal with the consequences. Besides, knowing he'd never be alone again was good. Whenever he left his bedroom—which so far had only been a few times—there was someone around to keep an eye on him and keep him company. He was getting to know every clan member and the psychics who now lived with them. It was a lot of people and overwhelming, but it also felt good.

He wasn't alone anymore.

Kenneth hovered next to him as he slowly made his way toward the stairs. He wasn't sure he'd have the strength to climb down, but maybe he'd find someone willing to carry him. The dragons all seemed eager to do just that when he needed it, and while it had embarrassed him the first few times, he was getting used to that, too. Clearly, they just wanted to spend time getting to know him and considered him part of the clan. That meant they wanted him to be part of clan life, and that wouldn't happen if he stayed in his bedroom.

"I'm glad you're here," Kenneth said as they reached the top of the stairs. "And your young man. I missed having company."

Just like it hadn't been easy for Valerian to be alone for seven years, it couldn't have been easy for Kenneth to be here and watch his family grow without being able to tell them he could see them. He'd died a while ago, but he'd never left, and he'd been alone the entire time.

Not anymore. Neither he nor Valerian was alone, and that was good.

Valerian grinned at him. "Maybe you can teach him some ghostly stuff."

Kenneth snorted. "I don't think there's anything I can teach him. He'll become stronger in time." Kenneth eyed Valerian. "Although when you have time, I'd like to talk to you about something."

Valerian wasn't surprised. "The corporeal thing."

"Yes. I'm not asking you to do it with me if you're uncomfortable, but I'd do pretty much anything to touch my wife again. I want to hug Tim and Victor. There's so much I've missed, even though I was here."

Valerian wasn't sure what to say. He wanted to comfort Kenneth, but how could he? He couldn't even begin to imagine what Kenneth's life had been like. "As soon as I'm better, we can talk about all of that," he promised. "I'll do what I can to make it happen."

Kenneth's smile was quick. "As long as you don't hurt yourself. Cooper and I don't need another ghost around the house."

"Hey there," a woman said as she came up behind Valerian.

He looked at her, expecting her to be staring at him because he'd been talking on his own, at least to her eyes, but she was smiling. Everyone knew that Kenneth was still around, and with the psychics in the house, the dragons were probably used to seeing them talking to empty spaces.

Valerian smiled. "Hi."

"You need help getting down the stairs?"

"It would be great. If you could just give me your arm or something."

"There's no need to take my arm." She leaned down and hauled Valerian into her arms. He squeaked and clung to her shoulders, sure she'd drop him, but she was strong.

He swallowed. From what he'd seen, most of the dragons were tall and well-built. Even the women were taller than he was, and they weren't ashamed of showing how strong they were. He wouldn't have been either, in their place. He felt a bit embarrassed that he was so short and scrawny.

"I'm Heloise," she said as she walked down the stairs.

"Thank you for telling me. It's hard to keep everyone in order when there are so many of you."

She chuckled. "No worries. Now, where should I put you down?"

Valerian wasn't offended at the fact that she was manhandling him like he was a child. He felt a bit like one but was grateful for the help. Every time he felt ashamed or embarrassed that he needed so much of it, he reminded himself that he wasn't alone anymore, and that was all that mattered.

The clan loved him in a way no one but his parents ever had, and Valerian would do everything in his power never to lose that, including allowing the dragons to carry him around the house.

Cooper was in the living room watching his brother and the other psychics work when someone walked in. He turned to find one of the dragons carrying Valerian into the room, and he pushed away from the wall he'd been leaning against. Valerian's expression told Cooper that he was embarrassed, but he was also smiling.

"Are you joining us for training?" York asked when he saw Valerian.

The dragon, whose name was Heloise, if Cooper remembered right, gently put Valerian down on an empty spot on the couch.

"He hasn't been cleared for training," Victor said, but he was smiling.

Even though Valerian hadn't been cleared for training, he *had* been cleared to leave his bedroom and start walking around on his own. He couldn't get far yet, which probably was why Heloise had carried him into the room, but it was obvious his newfound freedom had done him a lot of good. These days, he was more relaxed and slept better, even with the nightmares plaguing every single night.

There was nothing Cooper could do to get rid of them. He was tempted to seek out Curt and hurt him, but there were so many problems with that plan that he'd given up. Besides, hurting Curt wouldn't change anything when it came to Valerian's nightmares. They weren't because he was afraid Curt would find him, although that might be part of it. Most of all, he had nightmares because of what had already been done to him, and there was no changing that.

The group of psychics welcomed Valerian. Cooper stayed where he was, not wanting to interrupt. Valerian needed friends, especially friends who were alive. They could give him things Cooper couldn't, and while it hurt to admit it, Cooper had to. He had his limits, like everyone else. He wasn't the only person in Valerian's life anymore, and hopefully, that would be good for Valerian.

Valerian had noticed Cooper, of course, but beyond a smile, he didn't talk to him. Heloise left, and the psychics started working again. Valerian stayed out of the training, but he had a few tips that seemed to impress Victor, to the point that Victor started peppering him with questions. The other psychics quickly realized that meant the training session was over, and York didn't waste any time getting to his feet and coming closer to Cooper.

Cooper watched him move, yearning to touch his brother. He wanted to pull York into his arms and hug him, tell him that everything would be right now they were together again. He couldn't, but that didn't mean he couldn't be there for his brother.

"I like him," York said as he leaned against the wall next to Cooper.

"He's a good person."

"I'm glad you had him."

"It's more that we had each other." Cooper was pretty sure he'd have continued drifting if he hadn't met Valerian. He'd been in shock from his death and hadn't quite known who he was or what he was doing. Having Valerian need him had made him feel more alive, even though he wasn't. It had made him feel useful, which was what he'd needed to get out of that funk.

"Well, it's good to see you happy. I can't say I expected to find you like that when I got you back, but it's good."

"You never lost hope, did you?"

"Never. I knew you wouldn't leave me, which meant you were out there somewhere. I just had to find you." York chuckled. "I didn't expect it to happen like this, but how it happened doesn't matter. I have you back, and that's all I care about."

The urge to reach out to York was strong, but Cooper fought it. He didn't want his brother to feel bad about the fact that they couldn't touch. They couldn't have the relationship they'd had before, but they'd adapt the way they had when their parents had died. As long as they were together, they could do anything.

The smile on York's lips made it all worth it. It didn't matter that Cooper was painfully aware of the fact that he was dead and that a lot of the time, it hurt not to truly be part of the life of the people around him. The psychics had been welcoming, and they treated him like he was one of them, but he wasn't, and it was hard to ignore that sometimes. It was especially hard when he spent time with York.

"Are you going to ask him?" York asked.

"Ask who what?"

York rolled his eyes. "As if you don't know I'm talking about Valerian."

"I thought you were, but I couldn't be sure. What do you think I should be asking him?"

"If he can make you corporeal again."

"He does every time we touch."

York nodded curtly. "I just really want to hug you. I didn't think I'd ever get you back, and now I do, and I can't hug you."

Cooper didn't know if he still had a heart. He didn't have a body, so probably not, but it still broke at his brother's words. "We'll ask him once he's stronger," he promised.

York grinned. "Of course. And who knows, maybe he's

powerful enough to bring you back."

Cooper laughed. "I'm *dead*, Cooper. I'm never coming back as anything but a ghost."

York wasn't laughing. Something in his gaze told Cooper something was on his mind, but he was almost afraid to ask.

"I don't know," York whispered.

"I'm dead. I'm happy to be back with you, but you need to accept that."

"I have accepted it. I've been without you for too long to be able to ignore it. But think about it. Valerian is powerful enough that Curt and the cockatrices kidnapped him and were planning to use him. We don't know what Curt wanted with him, but what if Valerian can give you your life back?"

"Don't. No one can bring the dead back to life."

"Maybe not bring you back, but allow you to be corporeal even without touching him. I think that's possible. I asked Victor, and he's not sure, but there aren't many psychic mages around. Valerian has powers none of us can imagine, and I don't want to give up the hope that you could come back until he tells me there's nothing he can do."

Cooper understood where his brother was coming from. Hell, he felt the same way. He wanted to come back, too. He wanted to truly be a part of the lives the people around him were living, to hug his brother whenever he felt like it, and maybe even to kiss Valerian.

But thinking about this wasn't helping. It would only make things harder for him in the long run, which wasn't something he could deal with. It was better for him to focus on what he had rather than obsess over something that would probably never come true.

But he couldn't find it in himself to tell his brother to stop. York looked excited, almost bouncing on his feet, and Cooper found himself smiling at him.

Maybe giving his brother a little bit of hope wasn't so bad

after all. As long as Cooper kept in mind that he was dead and couldn't change that, it couldn't hurt.

Right?


Valerian had noticed Cooper and York talking, and it brought a smile to his face. Finding York was something Cooper had wanted for a long time, and Valerian was glad he'd been able to give him this. It didn't feel like enough, but Valerian thought it was a lot considering the situation.

Still, maybe he was strong enough to do more. Maybe he was strong enough to give Cooper things he'd never dared dream of.

Or he *would* be strong enough eventually. A strong wind might push him over right now, but that wouldn't last forever. He was eating regularly, sleeping without fear beyond the nightmares, and, more importantly, he was safe. He wasn't terrified of what would happen every second of every day, and that was helping a lot. He wasn't quite himself just yet, but eventually, that would change, and when it did, the first person he'd help was Cooper.

Because it wasn't fair. It wasn't fair that only Valerian could touch Cooper and that York had to wait for Valerian to be able to hug his brother. Valerian wasn't an idiot. He'd give pretty much anything to hug his parents again, so he imagined that was how York and Cooper felt. They were happy to be reunited, but it wasn't quite a full reunion.

"Not to be nosy, but those look like big thoughts," one of the men he was sitting with said.

Valerian turned his attention back to the group. He was still trying to associate names with faces, but the psychics were the easiest part. There weren't that many of them, and they'd made a point to keep Valerian company and be around him since he'd arrived. That was how Valerian knew that the one who'd spoken was Donahue, and the one who lightly slapped the back of his head was Olsen, his brother. Olsen wasn't a psychic, but he'd been born in a family of psychics and was always around. Valerian liked him.

"What did you do that for?" Donahue complained as he rubbed the back of his neck, even though his brother hadn't hit him hard.

"Don't be nosy."

"I just said I was going to be nosy. He knew what I was doing."

"It doesn't mean he's okay with it."

Valerian couldn't look away. He'd never had siblings, and sometimes, he wondered what his life would have been like if he had. It wasn't something he wanted to contemplate too often, though. Thinking of the family he'd lost and the opportunities he'd never have was painful, and it wouldn't change anything.

"I was thinking about Cooper," he admitted.

Donahue wiggled his eyebrows. "Have the two of you done the deed yet?"

Roslin, another one of Donahue's brothers, groaned. "Do you have to say it like that?"

"How else am I supposed to say it? I can't exactly ask him if he and his ghostly boyfriend have had sex yet and how it works, can I?"

Roslin spluttered. "Don't be rude."

"I was trying not to be!"

Valerian had to hide a smile. He'd never know what it was like to have brothers, but he imagined it would be very much like having these men around.

Victor sighed. "Ignore them, especially Donahue."

"Hey!" Donahue protested. "I was just curious. Aren't you? I mean, Cooper's a ghost, and Valerian can make him corporeal. Haven't you ever wondered what it would be like to have sex with a ghost?" All the brothers stared at Donahue. He stared back at them, then wiggled in his seat. "No? Just me?"

Olsen burst out laughing. "It would be kind of hard for me to wonder that when I can't even see them."

"*Please*, ignore them," Victor begged. "I'm doing my best to do the same. And don't feel like you have to answer their questions, because you don't, especially Donahue's."

"Why are you dumping me in with him?" Roslin asked. "He's the one who wants to have sex with a ghost, not me."

No matter how overwhelmed Valerian was most of the time, he wouldn't have changed a thing. Right now, surrounded by these people, he felt like he'd found home. It was exhilarating and overwhelming, and sometimes, he was terrified because it would be too easy for him to lose all of it.

But if he did, he'd fight to get it back. He wouldn't let anyone take the clan or Cooper away from him, especially not Curt and the cockatrices.

But obsessing over what they'd done to him and what they'd do in the future hadn't helped Valerian so far. If anything, it had made him even more anxious, which wasn't something he enjoyed. Maybe it was better for him to focus on Cooper and on making him corporeal permanently.

Valerian leaned closer to Victor. "I don't know why I can make Cooper and other ghosts corporeal, but I was wondering if I could make it permanent."

Victor blinked, visibly confused, but Donahue seemed on board with it, even though neither he nor Valerian knew what it would entail. He bounced in his seat, a wide smile stretching his lips.

"I'm sure you can do it. Would that involve making him visible to everyone?"

"I don't know. It's just a thought, but I'd rather think about this than about the cockatrices and what they did to me."

For a moment, no one spoke. Valerian had no doubt they were all thinking about what had happened to him, and while he didn't want them to worry, he was also touched. Before, no one would have cared about what he'd been through, but now, these people were doing everything they could to make sure he was okay and comfortable.

Victor cleared his throat. "I've never heard of anything like that."

"It doesn't mean it can't work," Donahue insisted. "I mean, I'd never seen anyone make ghosts corporeal the way he can. Who's to say he can't do more? If he can do that while exhausted and starved, imagine what will happen when he fully recovers." Donahue turned his beaming smile to Valerian. "I can't wait to see it."

Valerian found himself smiling back. He couldn't wait to see what he could do, either. Now that he wasn't on the run anymore, he didn't have to be careful, hide what he could do, or make sure no one ever found out. He could focus on learning how to use his powers and grow them. Maybe if he was strong enough, he could bring Cooper back. He doubted he could give Cooper his life back because he was dead, but maybe he didn't have to.

Maybe giving Cooper a chance to be corporeal again permanently would be enough.

And that wasn't all Valerian was planning on doing.

He looked around, his gaze stopping on the many people watching him. None of them looked afraid of what he could do or scornful of what he was thinking of trying. They'd support him through this, whether it worked or not. They were his family, just like the rest of the clan was.

"I want to try, and I want to help the clan. It's time I start."

"You need more rest," Victor protested.

Valerian couldn't deny that was true. He still felt weak, and he doubted he could do much until he could finally walk

around the house on his own again without feeling exhausted. He didn't know how long that would take, but he
had every intention of getting better and truly becoming part
of the clan.

And just maybe, giving Cooper a gift he deserved.

# Chapter Four

"You're doing great," Cooper said, and he made it sound like it was true.

Maybe it was. Valerian felt stronger, even though, at the moment, it only meant he was able to walk down the path in the yard on his own. Cooper was there to catch him if he stumbled, but he didn't think he would.

He was getting stronger. That meant that soon he'd be able to focus on helping the clan and Cooper and on growing his powers to ensure no one would ever be able to hurt him and the people he cared about ever again. It was as nerve-wracking as it was exciting, and Valerian couldn't wait to see what would happen next.

But before he could do anything, he needed to focus on himself. That was odd because he wasn't used to that. He'd been on the run since he was fifteen, which meant he'd needed to protect himself and ensure the coven couldn't get to him. His survival had been the only thing he could focus on, so he wasn't used to allowing himself to take naps and veg on the couch watching bad TV. Apparently, that was one of the ways he'd get stronger, though, and he was more than happy to do what the healer ordered, especially when Cooper was sitting next to him on the couch.

Cooper didn't spend all of his time with Valerian, but almost. He made sure to talk to York every day, and he was becoming friends with the other psychics, which was good to see. Just like Valerian, Cooper had been alone for too long. In his case, it was because he was dead, but being dead didn't mean loneliness or the end in their world. As long as there was a psychic around, there would be someone able to see Cooper, keep him company, and make him feel like he belonged.

"It's good to see you're getting stronger every day," Cooper said, looking away.

"It's good to feel like I'm more myself after everything I've gone through."

"I bet it is. Have you started thinking about what you'll do next? You're free to do pretty much anything now that the cockatrices are just a memory."

"You already know my plans."

"I know you're staying here, and I agree it's probably for the best, but I don't know anything else. Will you be working with the psychics? Or have you been thinking about leaving all of that behind?"

Valerian stopped walking. He stared at Cooper, trying to make sense of what his friend was saying. "What could I do if not work with the other psychics? To be honest, I think I should work with a mage, too, but I'm not going to ignore my powers or what I can do. It wouldn't be fair."

Cooper faced Valerian. "I don't care about fair. I only care about you and your happiness, and if you don't want to use your powers, you shouldn't have to. I doubt Elijah will force you to. He's a good person."

That much was true, and he wasn't the only one. Everyone who lived with the clan was a good person, which was one of the reasons Valerian was planning on doing everything he could to help them.

"I'll help keep the clan safe. I don't know how I'll do it yet, but after everything they've done for me, I want to do this for them." Valerian hesitated. He'd never asked Cooper this, but he'd been thinking about how to make Cooper permanently corporeal since the idea had popped up in his mind, and before he could start working on it, he needed to be sure. "What about you? Now that you know both me and your brother are safe, what are you planning on doing? Do you think moving on is something you might want to think about?"

Cooper looked like Valerian had slapped him, which wasn't what Valerian had been trying to do.

"Do you want me to move on?" he asked.

"Of course not, and you know that's not what I said. I don't want you to move on. I don't want to lose you, even though it's probably a bit selfish. I was just wondering why you didn't move on when you were lost." That was when he'd found Valerian, and together, they'd become stronger.

Valerian had needed Cooper to support him through being a prisoner and what Curt had done to him, but Valerian had been of no use to Cooper during that time. It would have been easy for Cooper to leave, and Valerian had often wondered why he hadn't.

"I couldn't leave York," Cooper said softly. "I knew he was out there, probably blaming himself for what happened to me and trying to find me. I didn't think he'd do something quite as stupid as helping Curt so he could get me back, but maybe I should have. We'd always been everything the other has. We were close even before our parents passed away, but we became each other's world after they died. I can see how wrong that was now, but I wouldn't change it even if I could. I needed York, and he needed me."

Just like Valerian needed him. He was pretty sure Cooper didn't see him as another brother. He certainly hoped that wasn't so, because he didn't view Cooper as a sibling—far from it.

"I'm not going anywhere," Cooper said, his tone telling Valerian how convinced he was. "I don't think I *could* go, even if you wanted me to. I hope that's not why you're asking."

Valerian quickly shook his head. "I don't want to lose you. You're my best friend and the person I love the most in the world."

Cooper's slightly guarded expression softened. "Same. Well, you're one of the people I love the most in the world. York is right there with you. I'm staying for both of you and because I don't want to leave you behind. Besides, I know what my life is like here, but I have no idea of what would happen if I did move on, and I'm not planning on finding out just yet."

"I can't help you there." Valerian didn't know what happened when a ghost moved on. He'd never died, and the ghosts who moved on never came back. No one could tell him what happened when they did, but he'd find out eventually.

Just not anytime soon.

He wanted to ask Cooper about his parents and whether maybe he could get them back if he moved on, but he was selfish. He didn't want Cooper to leave him, so, he didn't say anything about them. Maybe one day Cooper would realize just how selfish Valerian was, but in the meantime, Valerian would cling to him with both hands and never let go.

He wasn't strong enough to let go.

"I don't want you to leave, and I don't think York wants that either," he said as they started walking again.

"That's a good thing, because I'm not going anywhere."

There was humor in Cooper's voice now, and Valerian knew everything would be okay.

At least until they heard the voices.

Someone shouted, and Valerian and Cooper looked at each other. The sound of someone running reached Valerian, and he knew without having to ask that something had happened. What, though? Were the cockatrices attacking? It would be stupid, but Valerian wouldn't put it past them. Curt was evil, but he wasn't the smartest crayon in the pack, and from what

Valerian had seen, the alpha was used to letting him do what he wanted.

And if he wanted to attack the clan, he just might, and with the cockatrices' support.

Cooper didn't know what to do. He wanted to see what was happening, even though he would be of no help since he was a ghost. He needed to make sure Valerian and York were okay, though, which meant finding out what was going on. At the same time, he didn't want to put Valerian in danger, and he had no doubt that danger was at the gate.

That was where the screaming was coming from. It wasn't screaming anymore, though. That was just in the beginning. Still, Cooper could hear raised voices, and when he glanced at Valerian, he knew he wouldn't be able to keep him back.

That meant they were both going.

"You need to be careful," he told Valerian as they quickly walked toward the gate. "Maybe try to stay hidden behind a tree or something. Whatever's happening can't be good, and I don't want you to be in danger. You're still recuperating and don't have full access to your powers. Besides, if the cocka-trices are here, I doubt you'll be able to do much."

"I just want to know what's happening," Valerian said. "I promise I won't put myself in danger. I want to see this fight with the cockatrices through, but I have every intention of liv-ing a long life."

That was good. Valerian didn't have a death wish, and Cooper was already dead. Hopefully, it meant they'd both be all right by the end of whatever this was.

When they reached the gate, Cooper's stomach dropped. There was a small group on the other side of the gate, and he didn't have to go closer to know who they were. For some reason, the cockatrices had decided it would be a good idea to confront the dragons.

Cooper wasn't surprised. They'd never struck him as being smart, not even the alpha.

"You need to leave," one of the dragons at the gate said.

He stood with his arms crossed, and it was clear he wouldn't let anyone through. The cockatrices weren't trying, anyway. They were staring at him, and Cooper took the opportunity to move closer. As far as he knew, the cockatrices didn't have psychics beyond Curt's girlfriend, and he couldn't see her anywhere at the moment.

"We're not going anywhere until you give back what you've stolen," the cockatrice shifter at the front of the group said.

The dragon didn't allow the asshole to get to him. He continued staring, his stance not changing, and one of his brows arched.

"And what would that be?" Elijah's voice rang strong.

Cooper turned to watch as the alpha swiftly moved toward the gate. He wasn't alone, but Cooper hadn't expected him to be. Two dragons flanked him, one of which was Leo, York's partner. The other one was one of Leo's friends, Jerome. He looked pissed, and for a moment, Cooper wondered if he was about to reach between the bars of the gate and try to pull the cockatrice through them.

That would be a mess.

"You took our mage," the cockatrice said, sounding just a bit less convinced.

Cooper drifted closer. He peered at all the cockatrices, and his gaze finally stopped on someone he recognized.

Terrence.

Cooper still wasn't sure what to think of the man. He was a cockatrice shifter, but Cooper didn't think all of them were evil. They did what their alpha ordered them to do, even when they didn't want to. The entire clan was terrified of the alpha and Curt, and with good reason. Cooper hadn't been with them long, but even he knew it would be better for all of them to obey orders than to stand up to their alpha.

"I didn't steal anyone because people aren't things to steal," Elijah said. He paused in front of the gate and stared at the cockatrices as if they were nothing more than dog shit on the bottom of his shoe. "And you should know better than to come here. This is our territory, and I won't allow you to put my clan in danger or threaten us."

"Just give the mage back, and we'll leave."

Elijah cocked his head and stared at the cockatrice for a moment. "Do I have to speak more slowly for you to understand me?" he eventually asked.

The cockatrice's face turned red, and Cooper snickered. He liked the alpha, and he could tell the man had every intention of doing what whatever was necessary to keep his clan safe.

Cooper turned his attention back to Terrence. He'd been the only person nice to Valerian when Valerian had been a prisoner. He'd brought Valerian food, and even though he hadn't been supposed to, he'd tried helping him after Curt had beaten him. Both Cooper and Valerian had been suspicious in the beginning, and to be honest, Cooper still was. However, he didn't want to dismiss Terrence as a bad person upfront. He'd done too many things that hinted that he might not be bad, especially since, thanks to him, York was safe and sound. It would have been easy for Terrence to stop them from taking back York and Valerian, but instead, he'd helped.

And he'd paid for it if the bruises covering his face were an indication of anything.

Terrence had been beaten up. Cooper wasn't surprised, considering how the cockatrices had treated Valerian, and while he didn't fully trust the man, that didn't mean he wanted him to be in pain. There was nothing Cooper could do to help him, unfortunately. Terrence couldn't see him, but even if Cooper were corporeal, he wouldn't be able to convince Terrence to leave the cockatrices. Valerian had tried, and Terrence had said no. Cooper suspected there was a good reason he couldn't leave, but he had no idea what that reason was.

"Our alpha won't hesitate to strike if you don't give him what's his," the cockatrice in charge of the group snarled.

Elijah wasn't cowed. He was still staring, and Cooper wondered if it was a charade or if he truly felt annoyed rather than scared. Maybe he did. Cooper was terrified, but Elijah was the alpha for a reason, and he wasn't facing the cockatrices on his own. Several more dragons had appeared, including Kenneth, who was hovering at the back of their group next to Valerian. The other dragons had arranged themselves in such a way that the cockatrices couldn't see Valerian. Cooper suspected they'd done so on purpose, which told him how much the clan cared for Valerian.

That was good to see. If Cooper and Valerian had been on their own, Cooper wouldn't have been able to do anything. The dragons seemed intent on protecting Valerian, which was all Cooper wanted. He needed Valerian to be safe, but it wouldn't be easy since the cockatrices were involved.

They were stupid enough to be here, confronting the dragons. They had to know that if they even as much as set foot in dragon territory, Elijah would make sure they would never walk again, yet they didn't seem to care. They were outside the gate for now, but Cooper wondered what they'd do if they saw Valerian. Would they try to snatch him?

"Your alpha can't own a person. That means the mage is free to do whatever he wants and go where he wants, and he's a clan member now. Tell your alpha that."

The way the cockatrice paled told Cooper he knew what would happen to him when he told the alpha the news. Cooper almost wished he could be there to see the asshole's reaction.

"Valerian is a person, and you kidnapped and hurt him," Elijah continued. "But no more. Never again, not as long as the dragons are here. You have already hurt too many people, and we won't allow you to hurt anyone else. Valerian doesn't want to go with you, and I won't force him to. Now leave before I decide you're too close to my territory and send my dragons to get rid of you."

Elijah turned and walked away as if he didn't have a care in the world. He'd dismissed the cockatrices, who looked pissed, but also worried. They'd have to return to cockatrice territory without Valerian, which wouldn't be good for them. Cooper doubted they'd thought they'd convince the dragons to hand over Valerian, but for some reason, they'd decided to try anyway. It was puzzling, but everything in this situation seemed to be.

And Cooper and Valerian were right in the middle of it.

Valerian had stayed at the back of the group, but he'd still heard everything that was being said. His heart was racing, and he was terrified.

For a moment, when Elijah had arrived, Valerian had wondered if the alpha would hand him over. He wouldn't have blamed him if so. Elijah's clan had to come before a psychic Elijah barely knew. Valerian would have sacrificed himself without thinking twice about it if it meant keeping the clan safe.

Okay, maybe he *would* have thought twice about it, but in the end, he would have done it.

But Elijah hadn't even considered the idea, or if he had, he hadn't let it show. Instead, he'd told the cockatrices to fuck off and that Valerian one of his clan members. That meant he'd protect Valerian against the cockatrices, no matter how many people he had to sacrifice in order to do that.

Valerian wasn't happy about that. He felt sick at the thought that someone might have to die to keep him safe, and he didn't want that to happen, but what choice did he have? It was either stay with the dragons and wait for the cockatrices to do something or hand himself over, and he was too selfish to do that. He was finally free from the cockatrices. He was never going back, not unless they dragged him.

And they seemed intent on doing just that today.

The dragons stayed where they were, glaring at the cockatrices, who glared right back. They were at a standstill, and one of the groups had to move. For a moment, Valerian focused on Terrence.

Valerian hadn't been surprised to see him there. As soon as he'd realized the cockatrices were here to get him back, he'd expected to see Terrence, because that was the kind of thing the cockatrice alpha would do. He'd know it would hurt Valerian to see that someone had been hurt because of him, and it did.

He wondered what would happen if he pushed past the dragons and tried to reach Terrence. Cooper was still hovering around the cockatrice shifters, but he couldn't talk to Terrence or attempt to convince him to leave the cockatrices behind. Valerian couldn't offer Terrence safety with the dragons because it wasn't his place, but that didn't mean he wanted Terrence to stay with the cockatrices.

He didn't. They were hurting Terrence, and Valerian hated to see it. Terrence was the only cockatrice shifter who'd been nice to him, even though it had been clear he shouldn't have been. He'd made sure Valerian had enough food to eat, and when he could, he'd warned him that Curt and the alpha were coming. It hadn't helped much, and they'd still hurt Valerian, but it had given him time to steel himself and be ready by the time they reached the room he'd been locked in.

Valerian didn't want anything to happen to Terrence, but it was too late for that. Terrence's face was bruised, and he looked like he'd rather be anywhere but here. Valerian couldn't see well from where he was, but he was pretty sure that the cockatrice shifter standing next to Terrence was there to make sure he didn't make a run for it.

He wouldn't. Something held him back, and he wouldn't be going anywhere until he let go of that. Valerian hated it, but he had no say in it. Besides, showing the cockatrices he cared about Terrence would make things worse for him. It would give the alpha a reason to hurt him even more, and Valerian wouldn't be part of that.

"Leave," the dragon shifter who'd been confronting the cockatrices when Valerian and Cooper had arrived said.

The cockatrices all stared at him. Valerian thought that maybe, they would, but he should have remembered they were stupid.

"Give us the mage."

The dragon shifter sighed and took his phone out of his pocket. He quickly texted someone, and Valerian held his breath, waiting to see what would happen next. Thankfully the cockatrices couldn't see him, because he was standing behind a wall of dragon shifters. He hadn't been sure what to think when they'd first appeared, but now he realized they'd placed themselves in front of him so he could be protected. He was touched, and he'd make sure to thank all of them once this was over.

But it wasn't yet. Valerian had no idea what was about to happen and was afraid to find out, but there was no getting out of it. The cockatrices were here for him, and if they were going to hurt the dragons, he couldn't hide his head in the sand. He planned to protect the clan, and he'd follow through with it.

He just wasn't sure he was strong enough to do that at the

moment.

Cooper couldn't help but wonder if these cockatrice shifters had brains. The one in charge especially seemed not to understand the obvious, even after Elijah had made it clear.

He wasn't surprised to see Elijah pause, look at his phone, and turn around. He'd barely reached the house, and he had to be pissed to have to come back. He was the alpha, though, so it was his job to deal with the cockatrice shifters.

He didn't come back alone. Cooper watched as Victor moved into step with him. They talked for a moment, with Elijah nodding as if agreeing with what Victor was saying. Cooper wanted to know what was happening, so he left Terrence behind. He wasn't learning anything new amid the cockatrices, anyway. Most of them were wary, but they had a job to do, and they'd be in trouble if they didn't go back with Valerian.

Cooper doubted anyone had believed the dragons would hand him over, not even the cockatrice alpha. He'd sent his people on a foolish mission, and Cooper hoped for their sake that he wouldn't be too hard on them, but the man was angry and frustrated and ready to take it out on the most vulnerable of his people.

The people who had to obey his orders and go along with what he wanted even when they disagreed with it.

Cooper drifted over to Victor. He stopped by Valerian while Elijah moved toward the front of the group again. Victor's gaze flickered to Cooper, and he nodded, but most of his attention was on Valerian.

"You should head inside," he murmured.

"They're here because of me. I need to see what's going on," Valerian answered.

His focus was on the cockatrice shifters, specifically, on

Terrence. They weren't friends in any meaning of the word, but Terrence was the only human being who'd been nice to Valerian when he'd been with the cockatrices. It made sense that Valerian was worried about him. Cooper was, too, even though he wasn't sure he could trust the guy. Valerian's heart was soft and gentle, though, and he wanted to help Terrence. Cooper didn't have to ask to be sure of that.

Yelling at the gate made him turn. The leader of the cockatrice shifters was facing off with Elijah, and two of his people were trying to climb the gate. Cooper could have told them it was a bad idea, but he didn't have to. The dragon shifters had been standing and shielding Valerian from the gaze of the cockatrices, and now, they surged forward. Cooper was relieved to see Victor grab Valerian's arm and pull him toward the house. This time, Valerian didn't protest. He stared back with wide eyes, and Cooper couldn't help but notice that Terrence wasn't climbing the gate. He knew what would happen if he did, and while he refused to leave the cockatrices, he wasn't a willing participant in the attack.

For a few moments, everything was a mess. Cooper stayed where he was now that he knew Valerian was safe. He was dead, and most of the people around him couldn't see him. While he couldn't fight, he might be able to get details that would be useful to the clan, so he moved back toward the cockatrices. He got there just as one of the dragons shifted and roared.

Cooper hadn't seen who had shifted, but the dragon rushed forward and grabbed one of the cockatrices who'd reached the top of the gate. For a second, Cooper thought the dragon would eat the other shifter, but instead, they just pushed them to the other side of the gate.

"Leave," Elijah bellowed. "This is our territory, and we'll defend it with our lives. We won't hesitate to kill if that's what's needed. Is that really what you want to do today?

Die?"

The cockatrice who'd been dumped to the ground was slowly getting up while the one in charge turned pale. Clearly he wanted to leave but was afraid of what would happen if he did. Cooper didn't feel an ounce of pity for either of them. He understood their situation wasn't easy, but they had options, like leaving the cockatrice clan. Instead, they followed their alpha's orders, which meant they were in the wrong.

The cockatrice in charge finally raised his hands in surrender. "We're going," he said.

Elijah glared at him, clearly expecting it to be a trick. Cooper wouldn't have been surprised if it was, but the cockatrice in charge leaned down to help the one who'd been dumped to the ground to his feet. Then, never looking away from the dragons, he gestured at the others to get to the cars they'd left along the sidewalk. A few tried to protest, but eventually, they obeyed, albeit begrudgingly. They were already in trouble because they couldn't get Valerian back. Running away wouldn't change anything.

Cooper, along with Elijah and the other dragons, watched the cockatrices climb into their cars and drive away. Cooper only relaxed once he was sure they weren't coming back, but he couldn't help but wonder what would happen next.

This was a desperate attempt from the alpha, and Cooper didn't quite understand why he'd done it. He had to have known the dragons wouldn't hand Valerian over. Had he been trying to see how strong the clan was? Maybe how many guards kept the clan safe? Or had he wondered what the clan would be willing to do to keep Valerian?

Either way, the alpha would have a good idea of what the clan was ready to do. Hopefully, it would get him to take a step back, but something told Cooper that wouldn't happen.

# CHAPTER FIVE

Valerian stared out of the window. It was raining, which went well with his mood. He wished he wasn't stuck inside, but at least the house was big enough for him to roam and not feel like a prisoner.

He'd had enough of staying in his bedroom, so he left it every morning. He still felt like he'd run a marathon by the time he reached the living room, but he was getting stronger every day, which meant it was time for him to finally step up and do his part. He doubted Elijah would see things the same way, but what the alpha felt didn't matter. The clan protected Valerian, and it was time for Valerian to start protecting them.

They'd been taking care of him since he'd arrived. They'd been involved in getting him free from the cockatrice shifters. If it wasn't for the clan, Valerian would still be with them. He'd probably have agreed to work with Curt by now to stop the beatings. His bruises had vanished, but he could still feel the phantom pain of the beatings he'd lived through.

But he was safe now. Everyone in the clan had been nice, and as they'd shown when the cockatrice shifters had come to their gate, they were ready to defend him, whatever that entailed. It made Valerian feel like he wasn't doing enough, but he wasn't sure where to start. He wanted to help the clan, but did they need a psychic mage who didn't know what he was doing?

"What's going on in that head of yours?" Cooper asked as he brushed a fingertip against Valerian's forehead.

Ever since the cockatrices had come to the gate, Cooper had

been sticking close. Valerian was glad because it meant he was never alone, and while it might have been uncomfortable if it had been anyone else, he knew Cooper, and Cooper knew him. More importantly, they trusted each other, so Valerian didn't have a problem with Cooper being with him twenty-four-seven.

Well, almost twenty-four-seven.

He sighed and pressed his forehead against the cool glass of the window. "I feel stuck."

"Want to talk about it?"

"I doubt it'll help."

"Maybe, maybe not. You can't know until you tell me what's on your mind."

Valerian sighed. "I don't understand why the clan wants to help me so badly. I know I'm officially a clan member now, but I wasn't before, and I don't get why they wanted me to become one so badly. I thought it might be because of my powers, but Elijah hasn't asked me to do anything. Anyone else would have in his place, especially after what happened at the gate." Valerian turned to look at Cooper. "I'm confused."

Cooper's smile was gentle. "I don't think you need to understand any of this. Does it matter why they're doing it?"

"I guess it doesn't, but I don't like not understanding why people do the things they do." Because when he didn't, he was lost and didn't know what his reaction should be. More importantly, if he understood why people did the things they did, he knew whether or not they were trying to hurt him.

"Unfortunately for you, that's how most human beings work. No one thinks the same as anyone else, and you'll go nuts if you try understanding everyone around you."

"I'm not trying to do that. I just wish I could understand a few people."

Like Terrence. Valerian didn't understand why he stayed

back. He and Cooper had talked about it, and Cooper was convinced he had to have a good reason. He was probably right, but Valerian couldn't help but wonder if whatever reason Terrence had, it was worth getting hurt, or worse.

When Terrence had been at the gate, Valerian had seen the bruises, and he'd known where they'd come from. When Valerian had run, the alpha had to have been pissed. He'd no doubt taken his anger out on the cockatrice shifters who'd been there, including Terrence—maybe especially him since he'd been the one tasked with keeping an eye on Valerian.

What was worth putting himself through all that pain and anguish? What made it worth it for him to stay back, even though being with the cockatrices would eventually mean his death?

Cooper gently squeezed Valerian's shoulder. "You want to understand the world, but you can't, especially when it comes to shifters. You and I are humans, and I think it's one of the reasons we don't get most of their behavior. You don't understand why they want to protect you, but you're a clan member. To these dragons, their clan is everything. They won't allow anyone to touch one of their members, and that includes you."

Cooper was right, and maybe it meant that Valerian should stop trying to understand Elijah. The only thing that mattered was that Elijah had welcomed him as a clan member, and like Cooper had just said, he and the clan would protect Valerian no matter what happened. Valerian loathed the thought of someone getting hurt to protect him, but even though he didn't understand why the clan would do this, he knew they wouldn't hesitate and that they'd be offended if he tried to stop them.

"Why don't you talk to Victor or Elijah?" Cooper said.

Valerian frowned. "What about?"

"You want to help the clan, and Elijah is the only one who

knows how you can do that. The problem is that you don't know what you can do with your powers."

Valerian scowled. "I can do whatever I want. I'm much better than I was when I first arrived here. I'm strong enough to protect the clan the way they're protecting me."

Cooper grinned and raised his hands in surrender. "I wasn't saying that you're weak or anything like that, just that you never got any training, at least not after your parents were killed. You said that."

Valerian smoothed out his expression, feeling guilty that he'd snapped at Cooper. Cooper only wanted the best for him, and he'd never thought Valerian was weak. Valerian was frustrated, but it wasn't right for him to take it out on Cooper.

"You're right. I only trained until I was fifteen," he admitted. "Everything after that was focused on keeping myself safe and running from the coven."

Cooper nodded. "That's what I was saying. You have a basic understanding of your powers and what you can do, and while I'm sure Elijah would be glad for anything you can do to help, maybe it would be best to talk to Victor first. He can help you make sense of what you don't understand, and maybe he can even train you."

"I don't know how much he can do for my mage powers. He's a psychic."

"Then maybe we ask someone else for help when it comes to your mage powers. Gunther is still around, isn't he?"

Valerian nodded. He hadn't talked much to Gunther, but Elijah had explained he was a friend of his and a mage. He'd insisted Gunther move in with the clan so he could keep him safe, but Gunther had a coven, and from what Valerian understood, they weren't happy with his relationship with the clan. Valerian knew how complicated it was, even though he'd never lived through anything like that. It reminded him of the situation when his father and mother had gotten together, and he wished he could do something to help Gunther.

"Then why don't you start with Victor and Gunther? Talk to them. Ask them if they're willing to help you discover what you can and can't do. Talk to Elijah, too, and tell him what you're planning. He wants both of us to participate in clan life, and maybe you're right and it's time for us to start. I'm not sure what I'll be doing since I'm a ghost, but this is important to me, too."

Valerian leaned against Cooper. Cooper felt solid under Valerian's weight, and he always had. The touch thing Valerian could do with ghosts had always been strong with Cooper, and while Valerian didn't understand why, he didn't think it mattered. He and Cooper were a team. They'd survived together when they'd been with the cockatrices, and now, they'd found a clan and a place to belong, still together. Valerian had no doubt that Elijah would find a way to make Cooper useful, but Cooper wasn't the person who put the clan in danger.

That was Valerian, which meant he needed to do everything he could to keep the clan safe.

He was ready to do just that.

Cooper wasn't surprised that Valerian was chomping at the bits. He'd been feeling better for several days and wanted to do more for the clan. He didn't understand that the clan didn't expect anything from him, at least not while he was still healing, or why they'd want to protect him when they barely knew him. He didn't see how much the clan cared about him, and he thought that the only reason they could have wanted to keep him around was his powers.

Cooper had no doubt that was a part of Valerian's appeal.

The clan had kept Valerian safe against the cockatrices, and they would need help to push them back when they finally attacked. It wasn't a question of *if* but of *when*, and while Elijah hadn't pushed Valerian to do anything, everyone knew time was ticking. The near attack at the gate had exposed what the cockatrices were ready to do to get Valerian back, making Cooper wonder what Curt planned to do with Valerian. Did he need Valerian's powers or his ability to use them?

"I don't know what I'd do without you," Valerian whispered.

Cooper squeezed an arm around Valerian's shoulders. "Same."

"You're the only reason I didn't go nuts when I first arrived here. I like everyone, and they're nice, but they're not you." Valerian tilted his head to look at Cooper. "I can guess what Elijah expects from me, but I don't know what *you* want."

The words were on Cooper's lips, but he refused to let them out. Yes, he was in love with Valerian. How could he not be? The man was one of the bravest people Cooper had ever met. He was strong and caring, ready to sacrifice anything to help the people who'd helped him. He was sweet and gentle but wouldn't hesitate to strike the cockatrices if it meant keeping the clan safe. He was dealing with what had happened to him and his nightmares in a way that made Cooper proud, talking things out and understanding that none of what had happened had been his fault. It wasn't easy, but Valerian almost made it look like it was, and Cooper was in awe.

And very much in love.

But it wasn't fair to Valerian. Valerian was alive and should be dating someone who was, too. Even though they could touch each other, Cooper didn't think he could ever truly be part of Valerian's life. He couldn't give Valerian what someone alive could, and he felt it wouldn't be fair to tell Valerian about his feelings because it would only burden both of them.

But right now, looking into Valerian's eyes, he was tempted.

They stared at each other. Valerian licked his lips, and Cooper sucked in a breath. He had no idea what was happening, but he was powerless against the way Valerian looked at him. Valerian could have asked anything right now, and Cooper would have given it to him.

So, when Valerian inched closer, Cooper stayed as still as he could. He could tell what Valerian had in mind and knew it would be better to stop it, but he couldn't. He'd wanted to kiss Valerian for so long. He wanted to hold him, protect him, and love him. It was the worst thing they could do, yet Cooper couldn't find it in himself to stop it from happening.

So when Valerian's lips brushed against his, he leaned closer and kissed Valerian back. Valerian made a squeaking sound and pressed closer, going from zero to a hundred in seconds. It was as if he was afraid that if he didn't kiss Cooper now, he'd never get the opportunity to do it again. Cooper wanted to tell him to slow down, but he couldn't help but think that maybe, Valerian was right.

"Oh my god," someone yelped.

Cooper tore away from Valerian, but Valerian wasn't having any of that. He clung to Cooper, not allowing him to put distance between them.

"I'm sorry," Olsen said as he stared at them from the living room door. He rubbed the back of his neck, his expression sheepish. "I just needed a book I left here. I didn't mean to intrude."

"It's fine," Valerian reassured him with a smile.

Olsen hesitated. "You were kissing Cooper, weren't you?"

"I was," Valerian confirmed as if it were the most natural thing in the world.

Cooper wanted it to be.

"I'm happy for both of you. Can I just say how weird it was to walk in on that? I mean, I know Cooper's there, even though I can't see him, but you were tonguing the air."

Valerian's cheeks flushed, then he burst out laughing. Cooper snickered, too, as he tried to imagine what Olsen had seen.

Sometimes he wondered about Olsen. It couldn't be easy for him to be the only non-psychic in a psychic family, yet he never showed any discontent about his situation. He wasn't a psychic, but he was here with his brothers, and every time there was a meeting about how to deal with the cockatrices and Curt, he was present and didn't hesitate to speak up. He belonged with the clan, too, and he'd accepted it more easily than Valerian.

Olsen grinned." Well, even though it was weird for me, I'm happy for the two of you. It was about time you got your heads out of your asses. Even I could tell how much you care about each other, and I can't even hear or see Cooper."

"Thank you," Valerian said in a soft voice that made Cooper want to kiss him again.

Olsen looked around, found his book, and rushed to pick it up. "I'll leave you alone."

Valerian pushed away from Cooper. "You don't have to. You're welcome to sit with us, even though you can't see Cooper."

Cooper expected Olsen to leave, but instead, the man nodded and went to sit next to Valerian. He was a bit tense, which was understandable considering the situation. It wasn't easy for Cooper to communicate with someone who couldn't see him, and it couldn't be easy for Olsen to know he was there when he was unable to see him. Olsen always made an effort to include Cooper in the conversation, though, and Cooper was grateful for that.

"What were the two of you up to except the obvious?"

Olsen asked.

Valerian's cheeks were still flushed, but he grinned. "We were talking about what we can do for the clan."

Olsen nodded as if he understood, and maybe he did. "You think you're strong enough to use your powers now?"

"I think so, but the problem is that I don't know *how* to use them. My mother died before she could teach me most of what a mage's power can do, and as we know, I'm kind of special even for mages."

"You should probably talk to Gunther."

"That's what Cooper was telling me."

"Well, he had the right idea. No one else here will be able to help you when it comes to your mage powers, and as to what you can do to help the clan, you should talk to Elijah. He'll be able to tell you what the clan needs, and between him and Gunther, they can come up with a plan."

Valerian leaned closer, and Cooper watched him and Olsen as they talked. For a long time, Cooper had been the center of Valerian's world. They hadn't had a choice because Valerian had been a prisoner, but it felt good to see him spread his wings and finally start living his life.

What he'd had before, living on the run from his coven, hadn't been a life. He'd been alone and desperate, and that wasn't conducive to living. Here, with the clan, Valerian could have anything he wanted. The clan could become a family, which was what Cooper hoped for.

He didn't know what would happen between him and Valerian or with the cockatrices, but he felt better knowing that the clan would be there for Valerian and would protect him, even when Cooper couldn't. He wasn't the only one worried about Valerian anymore. The entire clan was, and that was a good thing.

# CHAPTER SIX

Valerian had been thinking about his abilities as a mage a lot lately. Before, he hadn't had the brain space to do so. His entire focus had been on surviving and not allowing the coven to get to him, then just on surviving after Curt had caught him. He'd never had time to sit down and think about what he could do and how strange it was.

As far as he knew, no other psychic could make ghosts corporeal. That probably meant that ability was linked to being a mage rather than a psychic, and he wished he could ask his father. He hadn't realized what he could do with ghosts until after his parents had died, and he couldn't help but wonder if his father would have known.

But even if he had, there was no way to ask him. Valerian had never seen his parents after they died, which meant they'd moved on rather than become ghosts. Sometimes he felt sad and angry about that. He'd needed them, especially when it first happened. More importantly, he'd wanted them in his life.

But they were gone, and hopefully, they were happy together in the afterlife. Valerian would see them again one day. In the meantime, he needed to focus on the family he had.

Cooper and the clan.

Valerian wanted to help the clan, but his interest lay in Cooper. Especially now that they'd kissed, it was hard not to think about what would happen if Valerian could make him corporeal permanently. Was that even possible?

He tapped his fingertips on his notebook. He was sitting at

the desk in his room but wasn't quite sure what he was doing there. He'd been wanting to make a list of things he could do, but unfortunately, that list was still empty. The only item he could put there was that he could make ghosts corporeal, but that would be of no use to the clan. Still, if Curt had wanted him so badly, it meant he knew that Valerian was capable of much more.

But what was that much more? It was anyone's guess.

How had Curt found out about Valerian, anyway? No one had known about his abilities except his parents, and they'd died. They might have told the coven members who'd caught up with them something, but it didn't sound right.

Valerian didn't know what the coven had done to them. He'd never gone back, and while sometimes he was tempted to see the house where his parents had died, it was better to stay away, and not just because the coven might find him. Besides, he was safe here, which was all his parents had wanted for him. They'd be pissed if he left the clan's safety to stare at their graves.

He grabbed a pen and wrote *making ghosts corporeal* on the list. He stared at the words, then tried to think about what else he could do. He wanted to explore this ability, though. He wouldn't know where to start, but maybe Victor could help. Victor was a psychic, so he didn't know much about mages and their abilities, but that didn't mean he didn't know anything at all.

Even if Victor couldn't help Valerian, it would be better than spending the next hour staring at an empty page.

Valerian pushed away from the desk. His legs still felt a bit wobbly, but they weren't weak anymore, and he didn't have any problem walking out of his bedroom and around the house to find Victor. Everyone knew how much Victor loved the library, so that was where Valerian decided to start.

He crossed paths with several people on his way there.

Everyone said hello and nodded, and for some reason, they seemed happy to see him. That was still something he was getting used to. Since his parents had died, Cooper was the only person who'd ever been happy to see him. Well, Curt had been happy when he got his hands on Valerian, but not because he'd wanted to be friends with him.

Was there a way to find out why Curt had decided to come after Valerian? Maybe even to discover how he'd known about Valerian's abilities when even Valerian wasn't sure about what he could do? Curt hadn't explained his plan, but since the only thing Valerian knew he could do for sure was making ghosts corporeal, he couldn't help but wonder if Curt's plan had hinged on that. Maybe he'd wanted Valerian to make ghosts corporeal. What ghosts, though? And to what purpose?

Valerian was still thinking about that as he walked into the library. He blinked and looked around, smiling at the sight of Victor reading by one of the windows.

Victor looked up and smiled back. "Were you looking for me?" he asked.

"Actually, yes. I wanted to talk about my abilities."

Victor put down his book. "I was wondering when you'd come."

"I should have asked sooner, but between everything, I decided to give myself more time. If you're not busy, can I sit with you?"

Victor waved at one of the empty chairs. "Please. I don't know how much help I can be, unfortunately." He picked up his phone. "But I think I heard that Gunther was back. Let me text him."

Valerian didn't know Gunther twell, so he was a bit wary of him, but if he was going to talk about this, he might as well have both a psychic and a mage in on the conversation.

Valerian was surprised to see Gunther arrive with Elijah,

but they both smiled at him and seemed relaxed, which meant nothing bad was happening. There was a sadness in Gunther's eyes, but he didn't say anything about it, and Valerian thought it probably had to do with his coven. Valerian, of all people, could understand how far some covens would go to keep their mages with them, and his heart went out to Gunther.

"Victor said you wanted to talk about your abilities," Gunther said as he flopped into one of the chairs.

Elijah took the last one, sitting more gracefully than Gunther. "I'm just here to listen," he told Valerian. "I doubt I'll understand much of what the three of you will be saying, but Gunther and I were together, and I'm curious."

"You want to know how you can use my abilities."

"I won't deny it would be good to know what you can do in case the cockatrices attack again, but that's not my main interest. I'm aware how difficult life has been for you and that you don't know much about yourself. Watching as you discover your abilities and how far they can stretch will be interesting. You're one of my people, and your happiness matters to me."

Valerian had to press his lips together and stay silent for a moment. Once he felt he had his emotions under control, he nodded and turned his attention back to Victor and Gunther. "I've been thinking about how I can make ghosts corporeal. I don't know how I do it, but I think it might be the reason Curt wanted me."

Victor's expression was grim. "He's tried to attack us with ghosts before. It wouldn't surprise me to find out he was trying to build a ghostly army. Making them corporeal, yet invisible to most people, would make that army efficient."

"But I can only make ghosts corporeal if they're touching me."

"Are you sure about that?" Gunther asked.

"Actually, no. I just know that with Cooper, my ability is stronger than with anyone else. The only different thing is how I feel about him and that he's my friend." Possibly more, but that wasn't what they were there to talk about.

Gunther slowly nodded. "So that ability is probably linked to your emotions. Are you asking us about this because you want to make Cooper permanently corporeal?"

"I'd like to at least try. Curt seemed to believe I could do it, and while I hate him and everything he stands for, I'd be interested in finding out if he was right. I just don't know where to start."

Valerian had only mentioned this to Cooper a few times because he didn't want to give Cooper false hope. Besides, this would be of no use to the clan.

"I can focus on other abilities I might have," he told Elijah. "I've only been focused on surviving since my parents died, but I'm sure I can be useful to the clan with some training and guidance."

Elijah shook his head. "I want you to focus on making ghosts corporeal. It's important to you, and I believe that figuring this out will open the way to your other abilities. You need to learn, and that's what I want you to do. It doesn't matter where you start."

Valerian leaned back in his chair. It was hard to believe Elijah, but on this occasion, he decided he would. He'd make Cooper corporeal permanently, no matter how long it took him to make it happen.

Cooper hadn't meant to listen to Valerian's conversation with Victor, Elijah, and Gunther. He and York had been browsing the library shelves and talking, and neither of them had realized Victor wasn't alone anymore until they heard more voices. Cooper could have left easily enough, even with

Victor and Valerian being able to see him, but York was another matter, so they'd decided to head to the other side of the room. Even then, they'd both heard what Valerian wanted to do, and Cooper's mind reeled at the thought.

Was what Valerian had said possible? Cooper had never heard of anything like that, but he hadn't been dead long, and apart from Kenneth, he'd never been friends with another ghost. He'd died recently enough that the one person who'd been in his life when he was alive was years away from dying.

"Can he do that?" York asked in a whisper.

His eyes were wide, and Cooper wanted to say yes. He wanted to tell his brother that he could have him back, albeit not the same as before. That was what Valerian was saying, wasn't it? That he could somehow make Cooper corporeal enough that he'd be able to hug his brother even without Valerian.

"I don't know." That was all Cooper could say, because he truly didn't know.

He was afraid to hope. He didn't know what being corporeal permanently would mean, if people other than psychics would be able to see him or if he'd still be an invisible man, but either way, being corporeal would mean he could get half a life back. He'd be able to touch York and hug him when he wanted. He'd be able to interact with the world around him, even if people couldn't see him. He supposed he'd still be dead, but being able to touch things again and people again might be worth it.

Or it might not be.

Cooper had made peace with his death. It had taken him some time, and the only reason he had was that Valerian had needed him. Knowing that had forced him to focus on Valerian and his problems rather than the fact that he was dead, and while it hadn't been easy, Cooper was fine with being dead now.

Well, mostly. He still hated that he was dead and wished he weren't, but he had his brother back, and he had Valerian. That was all he wanted in life. He didn't need to be alive to have them, which meant that he was fine with being deceased as long as he didn't move on.

But there was a spark in York's gaze, and Cooper knew his brother wouldn't let this go. Now that he'd heard the conversation, he seemed convinced he'd get Cooper back the way he was before, and Cooper didn't think it was possible, even if Valerian could, by some miracle, do this. He didn't want to let York know that, but he might have to.

"Don't get too excited," he tried to caution his brother.

York rolled his eyes. "You've always seen the glass half empty."

"That's because if you see it as half empty, you won't be disappointed when you realize it is."

York leaned closer. He reached for Cooper, but he stopped before trying to touch him. His hand would've gone right through Cooper if he'd tried, and the flash of pain on his face made Cooper want to hug him.

If he became permanently corporeal, he'd be able to do it.

York huffed and dropped his hand. "I get it. You don't want me to hope and be disappointed if it turns out that Valerian can't do it. I understand why you feel that way, but I can't help but hope. I could have you back, Cooper. It's all I've ever wanted since I lost you, and I'm not giving up that dream. It's fine if you don't want to believe in Valerian. I'll believe in him for both of us."

Those words made Cooper feel guilty. He should have more faith in the man he loved, shouldn't he? The problem was that neither he nor Valerian knew what Valerian could do. He'd been kidnapped by Curt, probably for his abilities as a psychic mage, but they didn't know what it meant. How would Curt have used Valerian? It could be his ability to make ghosts corporeal, but it could also be something else, maybe even something Curt imagined Valerian could do. Maybe the people who'd told Curt about Valerian had told him a lie or something that wasn't correct. Curt could have gone into this without knowing what Valerian could give him, and he might have decided to get rid of him once that happened.

But Valerian was safe, far away from Curt. The fact that the cockatrices had turned up on their doorstep wasn't great, but they hadn't done any damage. They'd yelled for a bit, then left with their tail between their legs.

Did cockatrice shifters have a tail?

Cooper didn't know, and he didn't care. He just cared about his family and the people he loved, and he couldn't stop thinking about Valerian's plan. Did Cooper want to become corporeal again? Of course he did. He'd give up pretty much anything to make that happen, and he didn't have much, to begin with. As a ghost, he didn't need a place to sleep. He didn't need food or anything material. He just drifted through life, but Valerian might be able to change that.

Cooper wanted it, and not just for himself. He wanted it for York's sake.

He was bouncing on the balls of his feet, leaning closer to the shelf as if to hear better what was being said. He truly believed Valerian could do this, and even though he'd told himself not to hope, Cooper found himself doing just that.

It wasn't just York. If Cooper was corporeal, he could help the clan. He could keep Valerian safe.

He and Valerian could truly be together.

If Cooper still had a heart, it would have been racing. He still felt emotions, even though he didn't have the physical properties, and he found himself getting excited. If Valerian truly could do this, it would be life-changing. It would mean that even though Cooper was dead, he'd still be here. He and

Valerian could be together like any other couple.

Cooper hadn't allowed himself to think about that because he'd never thought it possible, but now, he did. Valerian was offering him the world, and he wanted to take it.

# CHAPTER SEVEN

When he'd considered making Cooper permanently corporeal, Valerian knew it wouldn't be quick or easy. He'd known he would have to work hard to make it happen, find out what he could do, and use his ability.

He'd had no idea where to start, and he still didn't. Thankfully, Victor had agreed to help him, and Gunther had been almost as excited as Valerian. He was still dealing with his coven, though, so he wouldn't be able to be around much, but he'd promised he and Valerian would find a way to make it work.

Since Gunther wasn't here today, Valerian would start his training with Victor. He had no idea what to expect, but there was a bounce in his steps as he made his way to the library. That was where the psychics met to train, and for the first time, Valerian would be there with them.

His stomach churned with nervous excitement. No one would say anything if he sucked at being a psychic. That was good, because it meant Valerian didn't have to meet any expectations beyond his own. The problem was that his expectations were massive. He was aiming to make Cooper permanently corporeal, and he couldn't do it right now. He didn't know if he'd ever be able to do it, which worried him.

He'd told Cooper about it yesterday after talking with Victor and Gunther. He hadn't known what to expect, and while it had been obvious that Cooper wanted this as much as Valerian, if not more, he'd also clearly been trying not to get too excited. He probably didn't want to hope, which Valerian couldn't blame him for.

But he had to have faith in himself and what he could do. Maybe he didn't because he wasn't sure exactly what his abilities meant and what he could do, but that didn't matter. He'd find out soon enough.

He walked into the library, smiling at the sight of the men gathered around a small table. York beamed when he saw him. Victor and his brothers smiled, too, but it was more reserved. Lindsey was there, too, so it looked like Valerian would do this in front of a full house.

"Why don't you sit down with us?" Victor said as he gestured at the last empty seat.

Valerian flopped into it, telling himself not to worry too much. He didn't expect to succeed today. If it were that easy, he would have already done it. He already knew this would be long and hard, that he'd lose faith in himself more than once, but also that he'd get back to his feet and try again. He owed it to Cooper and himself.

Because having Cooper in his life that way was all he could think of. He wanted to kiss Cooper again, to build a life with him. He didn't care that Cooper was dead. As long as Cooper was here, they'd work things out. Valerian didn't even care if Cooper was corporeal. He wasn't letting him go.

But Valerian would have to convince Cooper of that, too. So he sat up straighter and nodded at Victor.

"Valerian and I were talking about how he can make ghosts corporeal yesterday," Victor explained to the other men.

"Is that something most psychics can do?" Lindsey asked. "Because I've never been able to do that. I haven't had much contact with other psychics except for my grandmother, so it would make sense for me not to be aware of this ability."

"It's not. As far as I know, Valerian is the only psychic I've ever heard of who's able to do that."

Lindsey nodded and relaxed. "Good. I thought I was missing something."

"You're not. We suspect it's the mix of Valerian's psychic and mage abilities. You and I, my brothers, and most psychics are just psychics. Our ability lies in seeing ghosts and being able to push them away and pull them toward us. Mages, on the other hand, have magic. I've never been close to a mage, so I can't tell you how strong their abilities are or what exactly they are, but I've worked with a few of them. Magic is incredible, and it's clear to me that magic, along with Valerian's psychic ability, is what's behind the corporeal thing."

"How do I make it permanent?" Valerian asked.

"I have no idea, but we'll find a way." Victor's smile was gentle and understanding. He obviously knew how important Cooper was to Valerian and wanted this for both of them.

Valerian was touched. He still wasn't used to people caring about him so much, but it felt good not to face all of this on his own. For once, he had backup and people who would help him.

"You can do this with any ghost? Or just with Cooper?" Roslin asked.

"Well, I haven't tried it with many ghosts, but both Cooper and Kenneth have become corporeal when I touch them."

Valerian had wanted to know, and Kenneth was the only other ghost hanging around the house. Thankfully, he'd been happy to help. He'd told Valerian that while he wouldn't want to be anywhere else, sometimes it felt like the days and nights never ended. It couldn't be easy for him to hang around the house and watch his family and the people he loved grow old. He wasn't part of their lives anymore, yet he was right there. Valerian had helped him hug his wife, son, and grandchildren, and they'd all been a mess after that. Kenneth loved his family so much that he'd decided not to move on until his wife passed away. When that happened, he'd already told Valerian he'd go with her.

But for now, neither of them was going anywhere.

Being able to do this for Kenneth meant Valerian could make any ghost corporeal by touching them. Now, he just had to find a way to make it permanent, but only for the ghosts he wanted corporeal.

"Let's see it," Victor said.

Cooper had been hovering at the edge of the group. He'd followed Valerian, looking skeptical but eager to be part of this. Valerian didn't blame him. He smiled when he held out a hand, and Cooper took it. Everyone around the table except for Olsen could see Cooper, and they stared.

"What's happening?" Olsen asked in a whisper.

"Olsen, why don't you touch the space next to Valerian?" Victor suggested.

Olsen stared at his brother for a moment. "Is that where Cooper is?"

"It is."

Olsen got to his feet and came to stand in front of Valerian. "Which side?"

"Why don't you tell me?" Victor asked.

Olsen was careful as he reached out. Valerian pressed his lips together because Olsen was trying to touch the wrong side, but he didn't say anything. He was curious about Olsen's reaction. He'd be able to feel Cooper, just like Kenneth's wife had been able to touch Kenneth. She wasn't a psychic, yet Valerian's presence and his touch meant she'd been aware of her husband for the first time since he died.

Olsen continued pushing forward, even when he couldn't touch anything. Cooper snickered, and Valerian waited. Eventually, Olsen huffed. "He's on the other side." He moved quickly, and this time, when he leaned forward, he did touch Cooper. His fingers brushed against Cooper's chest, and he hissed, then jumped back. His eyes were wide as he turned toward Victor. "I could feel him."

"That's because touching Valerian means he's corporeal." Victor looked at Valerian and nodded. "What happens if you let go?"

Valerian didn't want to, but he did anyway. When Olsen reached for Cooper this time, his hand passed right through Cooper's chest. Cooper grimaced, and Valerian's shoulders slumped.

"Please tell me I didn't put my hand straight through his dick or something," Olsen muttered.

The words made Valerian laugh, and he told himself he needed to stop being so defeatist. He'd known Olsen wouldn't be able to touch Cooper now that Valerian wasn't touching him anymore, and that was fine. It didn't mean this was impossible.

It couldn't be.

"He'd have to be eight feet tall for you to touch him there," Donahue pointed out with a snicker. "So no, you didn't punch him in the dick."

"Good. I did punch through him, right?"

Victor nodded. "You did, but it's nothing he isn't used to."

"Doesn't mean I enjoy it," Cooper grumbled.

Victor looked apologetic. "I'm sorry, but I'm not sure what I'm doing, and I thought this would be a good idea."

"It's fine. I'm just telling myself not to hope too much, you know?"

Victor's expression told Valerian he understood where Cooper was coming from.

Valerian squared his shoulders. He could do this, and he'd show everyone in the room that he could.

Cooper had expected to be disappointed, so he told himself it was fine. It wasn't like Valerian would suddenly wake up one day and fully understand these abilities as a mage. Right now, they were just poking at him and finding out what he could do. Once they knew, they could try to strengthen his ability to make Cooper corporeal and, hopefully, make it permanent.

Cooper expected it to take months, if not years. That was fine with him, since he was already dead. He wanted nothing more than this, but he'd need to be patient.

The sound of hurried footsteps approaching the library made them all sit up. It was never good when someone walked that quickly around the house, and Cooper wondered if the cockatrice shifters were at the gate again. There would be nothing he could do if so, dammit.

But it wasn't one of the dragon shifters here to tell them the cockatrices were here for Valerian again. When the door opened, Gunther breezed in, his cheeks flushed as if he'd come in a rush.

"Sorry, I'm late."

"You're not," Valerian told him with an easy smile. "We were just starting and freaking Olsen out."

Gunther looked surprised but grinned. "That sounds fun."

"It's not," Olsen grumbled.

Cooper had no idea what was happening, but he enjoyed watching Valerian smile and have fun, so he let it go without asking questions. He wasn't in a rush.

"How far did you get?" Gunther asked.

"I had Olsen touch Cooper while Valerian was touching him," Victor explained. "Olsen felt him, even though he's not a psychic, so the corporeal thing seems to work with humans."

"Does that mean I'll be the invisible man if we do this?" Cooper asked.

He wasn't sure he liked that idea. As it was, humans passed right through him. They couldn't see him, and that was fine with him. What would happen if he was corporeal? Humans wouldn't be able to walk through him, but they also wouldn't be able to see him. They'd freak out, which meant if this was how it ended up, Cooper would have to stay at the house and be extremely careful when he couldn't.

Gunther seemed to find Cooper's question amusing. "I guess you could be."

"That doesn't sound great."

"I understand. I can't make promises, but I'm pretty sure that Valerian's ability means that if you're fully corporeal, you'll be visible. I'm not saying you'll be alive again, because there's nothing that can do that, but you'll look alive enough to be able to spend time with humans."

That wasn't something Cooper had thought of. He didn't want humans to stumble against him when they couldn't see him, but he had no intention of spending any length of time with humans. York was a psychic, and he was here with Valerian. They could both see Cooper, so he wouldn't have to be careful about touching them. He just wanted to be able to touch and hug them and maybe to have the psychics in the house able to do the same. It would be a pity if the dragons couldn't, but Cooper could deal with that.

"Let's do that again," Gunther said.

Olsen sighed, but he obeyed.

Cooper lost count of how many times they repeated it. Gunther asked Valerian to touch Cooper more lightly, then harder. He asked him to focus, and while that caused Cooper to be slightly visible even to Olsen, it didn't make him corporeal once Valerian let go. He could see Valerian was getting tired, and he was about to tell him it was time to stop when a door slammed in the distance. Someone yelled, then he heard the sound of footsteps running.

Cooper looked at the others. They all knew it couldn't be good, and he could get there fast. He rushed out of the room, ignoring Valerian, who was calling out for him.

It took Cooper a moment to find where the noise was coming from. When he did, he wasn't surprised to realize that the person yelling was out of the house. The front door was open, and when Cooper walked out, he gasped.

Two dragons were on their knees, bracketing someone spread out on the ground. The gate was closed, but from the blood trail, it was clear the dragons had dragged the person on the ground closer to the house.

Cooper stepped to the side, his breath hitching when he realized the dragon in the middle was Heloise. He didn't know her well, but she'd been nice to Valerian every time they were together, and Cooper liked her. He couldn't begin to imagine what had happened to her and who had hurt her.

It was hard to look away, but Cooper wished he could. Heloise's long blonde hair was matted with blood and stuck to one side of her face. Her lower lip was cut, both of her eyes were swelling, and there was a long cut going from her forehead down to her nose. It crossed over one of her eyes, and Cooper wondered if she'd be able to keep it. He wasn't a doctor, so he had no idea.

Those weren't the only wounds on her. Long scratches covered her chest and stomach, clearly caused by claws. The t-shirt she'd been wearing had been shredded, and it wasn't hiding anything anymore, including the terrible wounds. What little fabric still covered Heloise was red with blood. Cooper was sure he'd seen her wearing a purple shirt this morning before she left for work, but it was blood red now.

"What happened?" Elijah asked as he pushed past the people who'd started coming out of the house.

Cooper didn't move. He didn't have to, since he wouldn't be a hindrance as long as Valerian didn't touch him. He wanted to find out what had happened to Heloise, but he had a good idea of the answer to that question. It could only be the cockatrices.

Everyone had known they'd do something. The alpha couldn't let what had happened go, and clearly, he'd decided that since he couldn't attack the clan head-on, he'd pick them off one by one. The first victim was Heloise.

"I don't know," one of the dragons kneeling next to Heloise said as he moved away to give Elijah more space. "We were guarding the gate when a car screeched by. It stopped long enough to dump Heloise in front of us, then left."

Elijah's jaw was tight as he nodded. "We'll talk again later."

Luckily, the dragons had a healer in the clan, and Irwin was pushing past the crowd. He gasped at the sight of Heloise, but he didn't hesitate to fall to his knees next to her.

"What happened?" he asked. "You know what? I don't care. I don't want to know what happened. We need to take her to the infirmary."

Elijah nodded, and together, they hauled Heloise up. She cried out, and Cooper winced. He didn't have to be here and watch this. He wanted to know what had happened and make sure the people who'd hurt Heloise paid for it, but he wouldn't be doing that himself. Besides, Valerian was there, too, his eyes wide and his face pale. Cooper needed to protect him, which meant taking him away.

"Let's go," he told Valerian when he reached him.

Valerian stared at him. "Who did that to her?"

"I don't know, but I can guess."

"The cockatrices."

That was the only answer that made sense, so Cooper didn't try to tell Valerian they couldn't be sure or that it might be someone else. They both knew that wasn't true.

The cockatrices had finally made their move.

Half of the clan had gathered outside the infirmary. The half who weren't there were either at work or guarding the property, but they all wanted to be present. Valerian was there, too, which was why he was pacing the hallway and ignoring the people glaring at him. They could deal with him needing to move, dammit.

He told himself it wasn't his fault. The cockatrices had attacked Heloise, and there was nothing Valerian had to blame himself for. He wasn't their alpha or the one giving them orders. The only people responsible were the alpha and the cockatrices who'd attacked Heloise, and that was that.

But Valerian felt guilty. From what Gunther had said and from the way Curt had behaved, he'd come to believe that he had incredible powers. He didn't know if that was true, but if it was, he needed to start using them to protect the clan. Instead, he'd been so obsessed with making Cooper permanently corporeal that he hadn't even thought about what kind of ability he might have that would help the clan.

He tightened his hands into fists and stopped next to a window. The people behind him were softly talking to each other, but he kept his focus on the trees.

He wouldn't give up making Cooper permanently corporeal, especially because he suspected that was the reason Curt had taken him. If Curt had been planning to use this ability, it meant it was powerful and that Valerian needed to control it. It wasn't the only thing he needed to do, though. He didn't know what kind of abilities he had as a mage, but whatever they were, he'd put all of them to work protecting the clan. He couldn't allow anyone else to be hurt like Heloise. It was a miracle she was alive, and while Irwin had promised she wasn't going to die, he'd looked worried.

Valerian was worried, too. He wanted to go in there and use his ability as a mage to heal Heloise and not even leave a scar on her. He didn't know if any mage in the world could do that, but it didn't matter. He just needed to do *something*.

"It wasn't your fault," Elijah said, suddenly appearing next to Valerian.

Valerian jumped. He hadn't heard Elijah coming, but he wasn't uncomfortable with his presence. They stood shoulder to shoulder, both of them looking out the window.

Valerian cleared his throat. "I know. The only ones at fault here are the cockatrices."

Elijah nodded curtly. "They're the ones to blame. They attacked the clan, and we can't retaliate." Elijah's jaw tightened. "I hate feeling powerless. These are my people getting hurt, and there's nothing I can do to help them."

Valerian had been feeling the same way seconds earlier, so he understood. "You can't start a war. It's what they want." And if a war did start, the humans would blame the dragons.

There was no proof that the cockatrice clan had been behind the attack. Valerian hoped someone would find something, but what were the odds? The cockatrices had to have known there were cameras by the gate, and if they were smart, they'd have made sure they couldn't be identified. But even if they could be, Valerian suspected the alpha would take no responsibility. He'd tell the human police force that one of his shifters had gone rogue, and nothing would happen to him. The corruption went too high, all the way to the chief of police. No one would do anything except turn against the dragons, and that wasn't something Elijah could allow.

"We'll make them pay," he murmured. "I promise you that. I don't know how I'll do it yet, but I'll find a way."

Elijah's smile was tight. "I have no doubt you will. I have faith in you and your abilities, even though I can see that you don't."

"What if there's nothing I can do to help? When you told me you wished for me to become a clan member, you explained that every clan member needed to be useful." And if

Valerian couldn't do anything to stop the cockatrices, he wouldn't be.

Elijah shook his head. "You don't need to physically protect the clan to be useful. You can find a job outside of the clan and use part of your money to upkeep the house. You can decide to work in the house, maybe cleaning or cooking. I don't expect you to become a guard or to use your powers against the cockatrices, although I can't deny it would be good to know we have a secret weapon. I just need you to be happy and safe, like the rest of the clan."

Except the clan wasn't safe. The cockatrices knew what they were doing when it came to the attack. They couldn't outright start a war, even though they probably wanted to. They could pick off the dragons one by one, though, weaken the clan, then finally attack. If they had the chief of police and the mayor in their pockets, they could do whatever they wanted to the clan, and the dragons wouldn't be able to retaliate or even protect themselves.

Valerian felt like he was the clan's only hope, but he didn't know what to do.

The infirmary door opened, and everyone straightened. The healer stepped out. He was drying his hands on a towel, and he looked exhausted. Valerian hadn't seen him like this since he'd arrived. He wanted to do something for Irwin, but there was no way for him to help.

"How is she?" Elijah asked, moving toward the infirmary door.

"You can't go in yet," Irwin stopped him. "She's resting, and she'll need a lot of that to get better."

"So she *will* get better?"

"Eventually. It won't be easy, and the road will be long, but she'll be fine. She'll have scars, and there's nothing I can do about that, but she's strong."

Valerian slumped against the wall, relieved. His gaze

caught with Cooper's, who was standing nearby, ready to act if Valerian needed him. Unfortunately, they were both powerless in this situation.

But if there was anything Valerian could do for the clan, he'd find out what that something was and use it against the cockatrices.

# Chapter Eight

The tension was running high, and Valerian didn't like it, or rather, he didn't like the reason behind it. Everyone in the clan had turned snappish and irritated, especially since Elijah had ordered that most of the clan members needed to stay home. Those who couldn't step away from their jobs still went out, but no one was to go anywhere on their own. What had happened to Heloise shocked the clan, and most of the members were afraid, but even more were angry and wanted to do something about the cockatrices.

They couldn't do anything. Valerian wasn't a dragon, but he shared their anger. He wanted to find Curt and make him pay for what he'd done to him and Heloise and to make sure he couldn't hurt anyone ever again. Unfortunately, it wasn't going to happen, at least not the way things were right now.

The cockatrices were getting more violent. They'd been attacking dragons left and right, taking advantage when they found them on their own or in small groups. Some of them were able to work from home, but most had to choose between safety and keeping their jobs. It wasn't right, but there was nothing Valerian could do for any of them.

Valerian's phone vibrated on his bed. He'd never had a phone before and was still learning how to use it, but he knew enough to open the group text to see what Elijah wanted. Whatever it was, it couldn't be good, but Valerian needed to know.

*Another two dragons were attacked this morning. Everyone is fine, but please, stay in clan territory as much as possible. If you lose your job, we'll find you something else and support you until all of this is over. I'd rather have all of you jobless than dead.*

Valerian dropped his phone back onto his bed and leaned back against his pillow. He resisted the urge to scream, because it wouldn't do anyone any good, not even him. With his luck, the dragons would hear him and run into his bedroom because they'd think he was being attacked, and he wouldn't blame them.

Heloise was still in the infirmary. She was recuperating, and Valerian had visited her. She'd seemed okay, or at least as okay as anyone in her position could be. She'd joked around with Valerian, her brother hovering next to her and glaring at him as if he was afraid Valerian would hurt her. Valerian hadn't stuck around for too long, but maybe he should go back now that it had been a few days. Everyone wanted to see her, though, and he didn't want to overwhelm her.

All in all, everything in Valerian's life was frustrating. He hadn't been planning to leave clan territory, but knowing he couldn't put him on edge. He'd been working with Victor as much as possible, but Gunther had vanished again, and while he'd been texting Valerian and offering advice, it wasn't the same as having him around.

Then there was Cooper. Valerian desperately wanted him, but Cooper had taken to being more distant. He wasn't avoiding him, but they weren't as close as before, and it hurt, especially because Valerian didn't know why Cooper was doing that.

Did he regret the kiss? Valerian didn't, and he had every intention of getting another one, possibly more. He wanted to kiss Cooper for the rest of his life, no matter how long that life would be. And, when he died, Cooper would be there, and they would decide what to do together.

But for all that to happen, he'd need Cooper to talk to him.

Between that and feeling like he should do more for the

dragons, Valerian was going nuts. He felt trapped again, even though it wasn't physical. He could leave his bedroom and roam the house or, even better, the area around it. The yard was well taken care of, and while it wasn't a forest, the small woods around the house was peaceful. Valerian wasn't the only one who often took advantage of the green space, but at the moment, he couldn't bear the thought of going out there.

He wanted Cooper. He was sure that some people would say their relationship was wrong because of how much Valerian depended on Cooper, but Valerian had decided to give himself a break. Considering everything that had happened throughout his life, did it matter that he was dependent on the man he loved? Cooper would never hurt him, and that was what Valerian needed. The only two people he'd ever loved had been taken from him. That probably was why he was clinging to Cooper with both hands.

Maybe that was Cooper's problem. Maybe he thought Valerian was too much, and he needed space. That was fine with Valerian, but if so, he wished Cooper had told him. He couldn't read Cooper's mind, even though he was a psychic mage.

He grabbed his phone again, hauled himself out of bed, and moved to the door. If Cooper didn't want to spend time with him, he could tell him. Valerian wasn't sure Cooper wanted to be with him, but if he did, they needed to find a way to make their relationship work. That meant talking to each other, and Valerian wouldn't let Cooper avoid it any longer.

Valerian was predictable. Usually, when he wasn't in his bedroom, he was either outside or in the library. Cooper was more complicated, but he tended to like the same spaces, and since Valerian was in the house, he headed to the library. It was big, with several nooks and crannies, and by the time he was done poking his head in all of them, he hadn't found

Cooper. Thankfully that didn't mean he had to continue searching, because Cooper and York came in as Valerian was ready to leave.

York smiled like he always did when he saw Valerian. "Hey. Were you looking for us?"

"For Cooper."

Cooper moved closer to Valerian. "What is it? Has something happened? Are you all right?"

It warmed Valerian's heart to see that Cooper cared so much. There had to be an explanation for the distance he'd put between them, and Valerian was about to find out what that explanation was. "I'm fine, but I'd like to talk."

"I'll go, then." York turned to his brother. "We can talk later. Valerian, why don't you come to the kitchen once you're done here? We can have a snack."

Valerian nodded. He liked York, and he loved that he'd been able to reunite the brothers. Even if that was the only thing that came out of this mess, it would have been worth it. He just hoped he wasn't about to lose his heart.

Cooper waited until his brother left, then sat in one of the chairs by the window. He leaned forward, rubbed his face with both hands, squared his shoulders, and looked up at Valerian. "What did you want to talk about?"

"Us. You've been avoiding me."

"Not exactly. I've been giving you space."

Valerian stomped his way to Cooper and stood over him, glaring. "I'd call that avoiding me. You're not talking to me. Well, you're not talking to me as much as before. You leave me alone a lot of the time, and while I understand that maybe sometimes I'm too dependent on you, I don't want to be ignored."

Cooper raised a hand. "I promise I'm not trying to ignore you. I just thought that it would be a good idea to give you space. I want you to make friends with the people in the house and to be able to live without me."

"Why? Are you planning on moving on?" If Cooper wanted that, Valerian would help him, but it would hurt like hell.

"No. I haven't thought of moving on, and I'm not planning to start anytime soon." He raked a hand through his hair. "It's just that you're alive, Valerian. You have your entire life in front of you, but I don't. I'm dead."

"Then it's good that I'm a psychic and have the ability to make you corporeal, isn't it? Because to me, it doesn't matter that you're dead. It doesn't change the way I feel about you." Valerian sucked in a breath. "It doesn't change the fact that I love you."

Cooper had expected the words, but they still stunned him. He'd known how Valerian felt about him, or at least, he'd hoped he wasn't seeing things just because he wanted them to be real. There was no way for him to ignore that Valerian had feelings for him, just like he had feelings for Valerian. But hearing him say it was like a punch to the stomach, and for a second, Cooper found himself unable to speak.

Valerian took that the wrong way. He stood up straighter, a scowl firmly on his face. "You don't have to say you love me back if you don't, but it's how I feel, and I'm tired of hiding it. I know things are complicated. I know I'm alive and that you're not, and that it might become a problem. Don't you think I haven't thought about it? Do you think I haven't thought about the fact that I'll grow old, but you won't? Whether I manage to make you fully corporeal or not, you'll always look twenty-two, while I'll look my age. Will you still love me when I'm forty? Fifty?"

"Of course I will. I don't love you because of how you look," Cooper reassured him.

"Every relationship is a risk. I realize I've never had one, but it doesn't mean I don't know that. No one can make promises. No one can say for sure what will happen in ten or twenty years. Hell, maybe *I'll* be the one to break up with you. Ever thought of that?"

Cooper had to work hard not to smile. He didn't want Valerian to think he was making fun of him because he wasn't. He loved Valerian and wanted nothing more than to kiss him again. There was something adorable in the way Valerian fought for them. When he was convinced of something, he did everything he could to get it, and clearly, that included Cooper.

Valerian snapped his mouth shut and stared at Cooper with wide eyes. Cooper got to his feet, wondering what had just happened. "What?" he asked, needing to know Valerian was okay.

"You just said you don't love me because of how I look."

"I did." He didn't understand why that shocked Valerian. Why did he think Cooper loved him?

"That means that you love me, just not for my looks," Valerian croaked.

"I thought that was obvious, sweetheart. Of course I love you. I've loved you almost since the day I first found you in that bedroom, bleeding and bruised." Cooper reached for him, gently touching his cheek. "I'm in awe of the fact that you love me. You're the strongest man I know, and I'm humbled by your feelings for me. I love you, Valerian. I realize I've been making a mess of this, but I felt I needed to give you space so you could wrap your mind around everything that was happening and make decisions. I didn't want to influence you or push you in a direction you weren't ready for."

Valerian stared for a moment. "You're an idiot," he eventually snapped.

There was no anger in the words, and Cooper found

himself chuckling. He pulled Valerian into his arms, and Valerian wrapped himself around him as if he was afraid Cooper would try to run. Cooper wasn't going anywhere. It was his fault Valerian seemed to believe he could leave him, and he'd need to make sure Valerian knew that wasn't the case. For now, though, he wanted nothing more than for Valerian to be in his arms.

So of course, that was when Valerian's phone started vibrating in his pocket. Cooper almost told him not to answer, but from the library, he could hear several more phones ringing in the house. That meant this was a group call, and they never happened unless something massive was going on. If Elijah wanted to communicate something to the entire clan, he texted. A phone call sounded like a disaster.

Cooper and Valerian looked at each other. Valerian didn't look afraid, but there was a wariness in his gaze that told Cooper he'd come to the same conclusion. Cooper wished he could shield Valerian from all of this, but he knew better than to try. Valerian deserved to know and to have a chance to defend himself, and Cooper couldn't take that from him.

Valerian stepped away and took his phone out of his pocket. He answered, putting the call on speaker. For a moment, Cooper couldn't hear anything. Then, the screech of metal against metal made him jump.

He and Cooper stared at each other with wide eyes. People were yelling on the other side of the phone, but no one was explaining what was happening.

The library door slammed open, making both of them jump. Cooper pushed Valerian behind his back and placed himself in front of him, even though there was little he'd be able to do to protect him. Thankfully, it wasn't someone attacking Valerian. It was Gunther, whom Cooper hadn't realized was in the house. His eyes were wide as he looked around, his gaze stopping on Cooper and Valerian.

"You need to hide," he told Valerian. He couldn't see Cooper, but it didn't matter.

"What's going on?" Valerian asked as he rushed forward, Cooper right behind him.

"I was out walking with Elijah when a car crashed through the gates."

"The cockatrices," Valerian said.

He probably wasn't wrong. They'd tried this once already. It wasn't surprising that they were trying again.

Gunther nodded and grabbed Valerian's hand. He pulled him into the hallway, and Cooper went after them.

This was one more reason he wanted Valerian to make him corporeal permanently. If he'd been corporeal right now, he might have been able to do something to protect Valerian. He wasn't sure whether or not he'd be vulnerable in his corporeal form or even if he could be killed again, but that didn't matter. He needed to be there for Valerian and the clan, and as it was, there was nothing he could do to protect them.

They met York and Olsen in the hallway. Both of them were pale and looking around with wide eyes, and Olsen was still on his phone. Cooper had almost forgotten about the clan-wide phone call, but he didn't need to ask what it was about. Hopefully, Elijah had managed to explain what was happening. The fact that they'd heard the sound of the car hitting the gate meant that Elijah was out there. What would happen to the clan if the alpha was hurt or worse? Cooper didn't want to think about it, because there was nothing he could do to change that. He couldn't go out there and protect Elijah or anyone. He was useless.

And he hated that.

"We need to get all the psychics to a safe place," Gunther said.

"There's a storage room not far from here," Olsen said. "It doesn't have windows, so as long as we can keep the door closed, we should be fine."

Gunther nodded and took his phone out. After unlocking it, he threw it at Olsen, then grabbed Valerian's hand again. "Text all the psychics and tell them where we're going. Don't hang up your phone yet, though. We need to hear what's going on."

Olsen obeyed as he rushed down the hallway. Cooper followed, even though he wasn't at risk. He wasn't leaving Valerian on his own. He didn't care what happened, but no one could take him away from Valerian when he was in danger.

Eventually they stopped in front of a door, and Olsen threw it open. The storage room wasn't large, so it would be a tight fit, but they'd make do. Olsen went in, putting his phone in his pocket as he did so, and pushed one of the shelves closer to the one behind it to make more space. Gunther followed his lead, then York. The three of them managed to free some space, and by the time the others started arriving, Cooper was relieved to see they'd all fit. They piled into the room, but as Donahue closed the door, the sound of something breaking in the hallway made all of them jump. Donahue hesitated just a second too long.

That second was just enough for the cockatrice shifter on the other side of the door to throw it open.


When the door slammed open, Valerian squeaked and stumbled backward. The others moved, too, all of them pressing toward the back of the storage room. The problem was that there was nowhere for them to go—there were no windows. They were stuck.

Right along with the cockatrice shifter staring them down.

The man was tall, with broad shoulders and a sinister grin on his lips. He looked from one person to the other, but eventually, his gaze stopped on Valerian. "There you are, little mage," he said.

Maybe Valerian shouldn't have been surprised that Victor placed himself in front of him, but he was. He didn't want anything to happen to Victor, especially not because of him. Victor was hell-bent on protecting Valerian, though, and it seemed like everyone else was, too, because they all moved as a group. They put themselves between Valerian and the cockatrice, and when York reached back, Valerian took his hand. He wanted Cooper, but Cooper was at the front of the group, even though he couldn't touch the cockatrice. So instead, Valerian took Roslin's hand and squeezed.

Valerian needed to do something. If he didn't, his friends would be hurt, and he couldn't let that happen. He was a mage, dammit. That meant he had powers, and he needed to use them *now*.

"Leave," Victor ordered.

The cockatrice laughed. "Why would I do that?"

"Because you'll get hurt if you don't."

That seemed to amuse the cockatrice shifter. "Will I? And how will you hurt me, psychic? You can see ghosts. How is that supposed to help you?"

"What I can or can't do doesn't matter. If you try to hurt Valerian, you'll have to deal with all of us."

Valerian was touched, but he was also terrified. He looked around the room, hoping to find something he could use, but he didn't know where to start when it came to his mage abilities. So far, the only thing he knew for sure that he could do was make ghosts corporeal.

He looked at Cooper. He was still in front of the group, glaring as if it might help him defeat the cockatrice. His hands were bunched into fists, and it was clear that he would have punched the lights out of the cockatrice shifter if he'd been corporeal. He couldn't, because he wasn't corporeal.

But he could be.

Valerian didn't know how they'd make it work if he had to keep touching Cooper for him to get rid of the cockatrice, but right now, something needed to happen, and he couldn't allow the cockatrice to take over and hurt one of his friends. He was already at risk anyway in the back of the group, , so he pushed forward.

He came to a stop next to Victor, with Cooper on his other side. Cooper glared at him and tried to tell him something, but Valerian ignored him. He didn't want the cockatrice to know there was a ghost with them.

"What do you want?" Valerian asked.

"For all dragons to die."

"I won't let you hurt them."

The cockatrice laughed. "As if you can do anything to stop us. I'm not the only cockatrice here today, little mage."

Valerian glared. "Can you stop with the *little mage* thing? You're not the villain in a fantasy movie."

The cockatrice's expression turned angry. "How dare you talk to me like that?"

York clung to Valerian's hand. Someone else touched Valerian's shoulder, but he was focused on the cockatrice and Cooper. He grabbed Cooper's shoulder, nodding at him when Cooper startled. Then he pushed everything he had into Cooper.

Valerian thought he'd worked out that this was how it happened. He made Cooper corporeal by lending him some of his power. The power seemed to like Cooper, because it went easily, but it wasn't enough, and as soon as Cooper stepped away from Valerian and Valerian couldn't touch him again, Valerian knew he wasn't corporeal anymore.

So he stepped forward and touched Cooper a second time.

The cockatrice was staring. Obviously, he could tell something was happening, and he was wary, but Valerian couldn't focus on him. He wanted the cockatrice to be afraid of him and his mage powers. *Little mage, my ass.* Valerian would show him.

Valerian pushed his power harder. He felt oddly energized and found that he could get even more power into Cooper than usual. When Olsen gasped, Valerian knew something had happened, but he couldn't say what. The cockatrice shifter's reaction was enough for him to take a wild guess, though. The man was staring at Cooper, even though he shouldn't be able to see him.

Cooper appeared as surprised as the cockatrice, but he didn't hesitate. He stepped away from Valerian, and Valerian had to let go. His skin buzzed, and he suddenly felt weak. He leaned back, knowing someone would catch him.

Olsen did. His eyes were wide, and he was still staring at Cooper. What did that mean?

"You can see him?" Valerian asked.

Olsen nodded. "And you're not even touching him. What did you do? How did you do it?"

Valerian shook his head. "I have no idea." And now wasn't the time to think about that. He didn't know if Cooper could get hurt. Technically, he was already dead. That meant nothing was supposed to be able to hurt him, but this was the first time they'd done something like this. Valerian didn't have answers, only questions.

Cooper yelled and threw himself at the cockatrice. The man stumbled back, hitting the door, but instead of stepping through it like Valerian had hoped he would, he jerked forward again, and Valerian watched in horror as the man started shifting.

Cockatrices weren't as big as dragons, but they were still big. That was probably the reason the man didn't shift completely. He wouldn't have fit in the storage room or the hallway. It would have been too easy for Valerian and the others to run by him while he was stuck, and he was clearly smart enough to realize that.

Cooper reached the cockatrice shifter as the man swung a shifted arm forward. He didn't have fingers anymore but rather claws, and Valerian watched in horror as they raked down Cooper's front. Cooper stumbled back, staring down at his chest. Valerian couldn't see what was happening there, but he tried to move. He needed to get to Cooper and make sure he was all right.

Olsen wasn't having any of it. He pulled Valerian back, shaking his head when Valerian tried to fight him.

"Look," he said.

Cooper wasn't falling to his knees. He wasn't leaning against the wall. Instead, he launched himself forward and punched the cockatrice shifter in the face.

Valerian gasped. Cooper wouldn't be moving like this if he were in pain, would he? Maybe the cockatrice hadn't hurt him. Maybe the claws had caught Cooper's shirt. It looked that way, but Valerian couldn't see much from where he was.

The cockatrice shifter stumbled back. Cooper's body did an odd flickering thing, and Olsen sucked in a breath.

"I think it's fading. He's flickering."

Valerian swore and tried to move again. If he could just touch Cooper, he could make him corporeal again.

Maybe. Valerian had no idea what he'd done differently this time, so he didn't know if he could replicate it. That wouldn't stop him from trying.

But the others wouldn't let him move closer. He turned to glare at them as a roar filled the hallway. Valerian pressed his hands to his ears, then turned to watch as a massive paw landed right on top of the cockatrice shifter.


Cooper tried to think about who was a red dragon, but the only one who came to mind was Elijah. Cooper didn't know if this was the alpha, but it didn't matter. The cockatrice wasn't getting up from that.

The dragon was massive, and it could barely move in the hallway. Still, Cooper watched as the dragon pressed his weight on top of the cockatrice, then winced at the sound of bones crushing.

That was disgusting.

The dragon quickly shifted, revealing Elijah. He looked fierce and angry, but when his gaze met Cooper's, Cooper saw his eyes widen.

Elijah stepped toward him, then stopped, his eyes widening even more. He turned to the rest of the men. "Please tell me that was Cooper. I just saw a man standing there. He was there one second, then gone."

Everyone was silent. Then Valerian pushed away from the others and rushed to Cooper's side. "Oh, my god. Did he hurt you? I saw him claw you, but you punched him anyway and didn't seem to be in pain. How are you feeling? Are you bleeding?"

He seemed afraid to touch Cooper, which Cooper could understand. He caught one of Valerian's hands, wanting to reassure him. "I'm fine."

"Are you sure? Because that looked like it hurt."

Cooper looked down at his chest. He had no doubt that it would have hurt if he'd been alive, but he hadn't felt much. He was dead, after all, even though he'd been corporeal when the cockatrice had attacked him. "I'm fine." He could see that the cockatrice had caught him, because his t-shirt was torn. When he pushed the fabric apart, though, his chest was just like it had always been. There was no sign of any scratches and no blood.

Valerian's shoulders slumped, and he pressed his hand against Cooper's chest. "Thank god. I thought for sure he'd hurt you."

"He should have," Victor said, coming closer to peer at Cooper's chest.

Cooper resisted the urge to cover himself. Victor wasn't looking at him because he thought he was attractive. There was a calculating expression on his face, and Cooper had no doubt he was already thinking about what had happened and how Valerian had done it.

"Is everyone all right?" Elijah asked.

Everyone nodded and said yes. Cooper could see they were still scared, which was understandable. He was scared, too, even though the cockatrices couldn't touch him. More than for himself, he was frightened for the others, for Valerian and York, for the people he'd come to see as his friends.

But everyone was okay.

"Cooper saved the day," Gunther said as he pushed forward. "I don't know how Valerian did it, but he made Cooper both corporeal and visible. It didn't last long, but long enough for Cooper to punch the cockatrice. Then you stepped in." Gunther wrinkled his nose and looked out in the hallway. "Quite literally. Do you know how hard it's going to be to get the blood and bones out of the carpet?"

To everyone's surprise, Elijah pulled Gunther into his arms. Gunther squeaked, and it took him a moment to hug Elijah back, but eventually, he did.

Cooper looked away, thinking this was an intimate moment they both needed. "How am I not hurt?" he asked no one in particular.

"I'd have to guess it's because you're already dead," Victor said.

He was leaning so close to Cooper's chest now that Cooper wondered if he was going to start poking at him—with his nose.

"But I was corporeal."

"You were, but you're also already dead. You can't be

killed again, and clearly, you also can't be hurt. Did that hurt at all?"

Cooper shrugged. "I wasn't exactly thinking or stopping to understand how I was feeling. I guess it burned for a moment. Nothing like what it should have, though."

"I want all of you to stay in the storage room," Elijah said, having stepped away from Gunther. "Several cars came in, and we're fighting to get them out again. I'm pretty sure someone called the police because I can hear sirens, but as long as you stay in this room behind the locked door, you should be okay." He looked at Gunther. "I need you to take this seriously and be safe."

Cooper wasn't sure if he was just talking to Gunther or to everyone, but it didn't matter. They all wanted to be safe, so they nodded and shuffled back into the room. This time, they did manage to close the door. Elijah made sure of that He locked them inside, and silence descended over the room.

"So," Olsen eventually said.

Cooper was pretty sure he knew what Olsen wanted to talk about. He wanted to talk about it, too, because it had been incredible.

He grinned at Valerian. "How?"

Valerian shrugged. "I have no idea. We already tried to push as much of my power as I could into you, but it never worked like that. I don't know what happened."

"I might," Victor said.

They could hear the sound of fighting in the distance, and Cooper was glad for the distraction. It made him feel selfish to focus on himself and what had happened to him, but if it meant Valerian was focused on him rather than on the fight outside the door, it was fine with him.

Everyone turned to Victor. He didn't seem to care that they were all staring at him, maybe because he was used to it. He'd been teaching the psychics since everyone had moved into the house, and his brothers trained with him, even though they were just as good at using their psychic ability.

"Do you remember who was touching you when you poured that power into Cooper?" Victor asked.

Valerian blinked. "I think you were touching my shoulder."

"And I was holding your hand," York added. His eyes were wide as he watched Victor. "You think that the two of us touching him gave him a boost?"

"That's what would make the most sense. We already know Valerian has the ability to make Cooper and other ghosts corporeal. Maybe he doesn't have enough power yet to make it permanent. I'm not sure how similar the powers of mages and psychics are, but we grow stronger as we age and learn how to use our ability, and since Valerian was able to use our power, I suspect they're similar enough. I'm ready to bet mages grow stronger as they age and learn, too, and we know this ability is rooted in Valerian's mage powers."

"So if he can use enough of our power, he could make Cooper permanently corporeal."

"My guess is that it might just work," Victor agreed. "He could wait and get stronger in time, or like he did today, he could use us."

York grinned and threw himself at Valerian, who caught him. They hugged, but Cooper kept an eye on Victor. He was smiling, but he didn't look as happy as the others.

"What is it?" he asked.

"I think it will work, but we have no way of knowing how much power Valerian will need to take from us. We might be enough, or we might not be, and in that case, we'd have to find other psychics willing to help."

Cooper understood where Victor was coming from, but he couldn't find it in himself to share his feelings, at least not right now. He had no doubt that later, once this mess was over and he had some time to think over everything, he'd realize Victor was right, but for now, he had a real chance at becoming corporeal again, and it made him happy.

As the dragons kicked cockatrice-ass outside the storage room, the psychics gathered and started planning how they would do this. Cooper had faith, both in them and in the dragons. The dragons would keep the clan safe and kick every cockatrice out, while the psychics would make Cooper corporeal again.

# Chapter Nine

The clan was safe. That was hard to believe once the aftermath of the attack was visible through the living room window through which Valerian was staring, but the cockatrices were gone.

Or at least, most of them were.

Valerian swallowed at the sight of the body on the ground and made a conscious effort not to look at it. Part of him was morbidly curious, especially because the cockatrices had attacked them, not the other way around, but another part of him knew the body had belonged to a human being. Did it matter that it wasn't a good person? Valerian couldn't even know that for sure. The cockatrice alpha had a death grip on his clan, and Valerian doubted any of the cockatrices who'd attacked the clan today had been given a choice. Some might have come because they'd wanted to destroy the dragons, but others had been forced to, and there was no way to know which group the dead man on the ground had belonged to.

Valerian didn't think the dragons should feel guilty about killing some of the cockatrices. They were defending their home, and while it made his stomach churn, he was very much aware that it would have been either the dragons or the cockatrices. The cockatrices had been here to destroy the dragons, and it was a miracle the clan was still standing.

Valerian hoped the police officers poking around clan territory thought the same. They'd arrived sometime after the fight had started, and when did, most of the cockatrices still standing had run. Valerian couldn't imagine why they were afraid of humans, but maybe fear wasn't why they ran. The cockatrice alpha clearly wanted the fact that he'd attacked to be kept quiet as much as possible. Valerian didn't see how that could work, but he supposed that with enough support from the police chief, anything was possible.

Especially because the mayor was involved, too.

There was a distinct possibility that the dragons would be in trouble for this, even though they'd been the ones attacked. Valerian didn't think there was anything he or anyone else could do about it. The police would think and do whatever they wanted, like they always did. But as long as no one ended up behind bars, Valerian thought everything would be okay.

Or rather, he hoped so.

Cooper's hand tightened around Valerian's fingers when they heard voices in the entrance. They both turned away from the living room window, and Valerian wondered if some of the police officers had had enough courage to come into the house. They'd been ordering the dragons around since they'd arrived, and Elijah wasn't taking it well. He was still on high alert after the attack, and Valerian was pretty sure he'd seen him growl at one police officer at least. The man had quickly stepped away, but not all of them were as smart as that guy.

"What do you think will happen?" Valerian asked Cooper.

Cooper grunted. "It's anybody's guess. I don't think the police can deny the fact that the cockatrices were the ones who attacked, though."

"They can try."

Cooper snorted. "They probably will. The clan doesn't need the human police force, anyway. We know who attacked, and we know why. We know they'll try again."

That was Valerian's worst fear. His friends were all right. There were a few wounded dragons, but no one from the clan had died. The same couldn't be said for the cockatrices, but Valerian couldn't find it in himself to care. It might make him a bad person, but those cockatrices had come here to kill the dragons and take him back. Was it that bad that he didn't feel sorry about their deaths?

Suddenly he heard a loud voice. "You need to come with us."

Valerian and Cooper looked at each other. Valerian didn't want anyone to leave clan territory, and they shouldn't have to. The only thing the clan had done was defend itself, but he wasn't surprised to realize that not all police officers felt that way. He quickly tugged Cooper forward, needing to find out who was being taken away.

It was Elijah.

A tall police officer was standing in front of him, looking like he wanted to hit him. The man's jaw was tight, and he was holding a pair of handcuffs. Elijah didn't seem to care, though. He stared back at the scowling officer, his arms crossed over his chest, silently telling the man he wasn't going anywhere. Valerian was relieved. He didn't know what the clan would do if Elijah were to be taken away right now.

"He hasn't done anything," York protested.

Most of the psychics and Gunther were gathered in the entrance, standing behind Elijah in support. A few of the dragons were present, too, but most were checking in on their families or cleaning the damage done by the cockatrices attack.

The police officers puffed out his chest. "That's for us to decide. You're the alpha, correct?"

"I already told you I am."

"Then you need to come with us. If you don't come willingly, I'll have to arrest you." He dangled the handcuffs from his fingers as if Elijah would obey because of them.

Valerian was angry. Did this officer think Elijah was in the wrong? The cockatrice shifters had attacked. Why else would there be a cockatrice splattered on the carpet upstairs? But this officer didn't seem to care. Valerian suspected he was one of those who didn't like shifters and didn't care who was wrong and right in the story. As long as he could have a shifter behind bars, he'd be happy.

"I'll come," Elijah said.

He probably didn't want to make even more of a mess of the situation, which Valerian understood and agreed with, but he wasn't sure this was a good idea. He didn't see how they could get out of it, unfortunately.

"You can't," York protested. "You haven't done anything wrong. They attacked us, and we defended ourselves."

"Were you involved in the fight, sir?" the officer asked. He looked ready to find another set of handcuffs for York.

Leo hooked an arm around York's shoulders and pulled him away. "He was locked in a storage room with his friends," Leo said, scowling at the officer. "He had nothing to do with this."

It was clear that if the officer tried to come anywhere near York with his handcuffs, he wouldn't see the next day.

*Good.*

"I'm sure this nice officer will realize York is right and that we were only defending ourselves," Elijah said slowly, looking from one person to the other. "In the meantime, take care of the clan. It won't be long before I'm back." He glared at the officer. "I have extremely good lawyers."

The man didn't seem to care. His face had a triumphant expression as he guided Elijah toward the door, although he seemed a bit resigned as he put away the handcuffs. Valerian rushed after them along with everyone else. It wasn't right, and he wanted to scream in frustration, but that would only put a spotlight on him, and that was the last thing he wanted.

A roar of noise met him when he stepped onto the stone steps following Elijah and the officer. For a moment, he wondered if one of the dragons had shifted, but then he realized it was the crowd in front of the gate.

The attack had been obvious, and most of the people who lived on the same street as the clan had noticed something was happening. Of course, that meant the press had found out, too, and it seemed like every journalist in the city was standing on the other side of the gate that was propped up where it had once stood.

Valerian steeled himself for how the press would twist the situation, and it took him a second to realize what the journalists were saying. When he did, he blinked, unable to believe what he was hearing.

"Why are you arresting the dragon alpha when the cockatrice shifters are clearly in the wrong here?" a woman asked, waving her microphone toward the officer through the bars.

"Shouldn't you be focused on the cockatrices?" a man asked. He pushed forward, stopping in front of the gate and thrusting his phone between the bars to get closer. "The cockatrice shifters were in the wrong since they entered dragon territory. Why aren't you investigating them?"

"Fuck off," the officer muttered.

The journalist seemed to find that funny, and he smiled. "Sure, as soon as you give me answers. People will want to know why the police are focusing on the wrong people. They have a right to know that no one is doing anything to stop the cockatrice shifters from attacking people they don't like. Who will be next? Another shifter group? The government?"

Valerian watched in awe as the police officer stopped walking. Elijah stopped with him, and while he looked surprised when the officer pushed him away, he didn't hesitate to step away. He looked from the officer to the journalist, then nodded at the journalist, who was still holding his phone through the bars.

"Can you give me an interview?" the man asked.

"Give me your number, and I'll contact you," Elijah told

him.

The journalist grinned. "I'm Paul Bay." He dug into his pocket and took out a business card. "Here are my numbers and email. I trust that you'll call me."

Elijah took the card. "Eventually."

Elijah would already be on his way to the police station if it weren't for this guy. That didn't mean he'd go along with what Bay was asking, but there was a good chance he'd at least agree to talk to the guy. Now wasn't the right moment, so Valerian wasn't surprised when Elijah turned to the officer who'd been taking him away. "What will you do about all of this? About the cockatrices?"

The expression on the man's face told Valerian no one would like his answer.

"There's nothing I can do, sir," the officer said. He sounded pissed, but with the journalists still yelling questions, he obviously couldn't afford to be disrespectful.


Cooper sucked in a breath and wondered what the man would think if Cooper were to punch him. He was still holding Valerian's hand, so while the officer was unable to see him, he'd certainly feel it.

"What do you mean?" Elijah asked in a deadly voice.

The officer looked cowed, but only for a second. Then, he gathered himself and squared his shoulders. "The only people we know for sure were here during the attack are dead. We have no proof of anyone else being here, and we can't arrest people just because you say they attacked you."

Cooper sputtered. "Isn't that exactly what the police are supposed to do?" he asked no one in particular. Only a few of the psychics had followed Elijah outside when he'd been taken away, and all were staring. They seemed to have the same problem wrapping their minds around what was happening as Cooper.

"Your job is to listen to the victims and investigate the crime," Elijah said. "Well, I'm reporting a crime. The cockatrice alpha ordered his people to attack my clan. They came into dragon territory and need to be punished for that."

The officer bristled. "You leave that to human justice."

"I'll be happy to do that, but I need human justice to do something about it."

"We know how to do our job, sir. As it is, there's nothing we can do to help you."

Elijah stared for a moment. "I see." He turned toward Bay. "It looks like you and I will talk much sooner than I expected."

The officer looked like he wanted to do something, like maybe arrest both Elijah and Bay, but he didn't move, not even when Elijah gestured at one of the dragons by the gate to let Bay through. Bay looked like a kid in an ice cream store. He bounced in and beamed at the police officer. Cooper was so startled that he almost laughed, especially when the officer stared at Bay as if he didn't know what to do with him.

"Thank you," Bay said, turning to Elijah. "Can you tell me what happened? We heard about cockatrice shifters attacking your clan, but I'd like more details."

"You can't do that," the police officer tried.

"Why not? This isn't your property. The dragon alpha can talk to whoever he wants, and unless you want to comment on the situation, I'd like to focus on my interview."

The officer's face turned red, but he didn't try to stop Bay and Elijah from talking. He had to know he didn't have a reason to do so.

Cooper focused on Bay as Elijah explained what had happened. He told him how the cockatrices had rammed several cars through the gate and how he and the other clan dragons had defended themselves and their home.

It had been a good idea to prop up the gates, even though they were twisted and only leaning against the stone walls. They were too heavy for humans to move them, and if the cockatrices came back and tried to sneak in through them, it would make enough noise for the dragons to notice. Cooper could only imagine the chaos if the journalists had been allowed to stream in. Several of them looked like they were thinking about scaling the gate, but they knew better than to invade a dragon alpha's territory.

Cooper listened as Elijah told Bay everything, including the fact that the police force had refused to help him keep his clan safe, even though Bay was right there when the officer told Elijah that. It was Elijah's job to protect his clan, but he'd been staying away from the cockatrices because he wished to stay on the right side of the law.

Cooper had no doubt that if the dragons had attacked the cockatrices, the police force would already be on them, carting them off to prison. Were they working with Curt? It sure seemed like it, and Cooper didn't know how the dragons would find a way around that. It wasn't just the chief of police, either. The mayor was involved, and between the two of them, they had a massive amount of power.

It felt like Elijah was playing with fire. He was giving an interview and being honest about most details, although Cooper didn't miss the fact that he never mentioned Valerian. He wasn't shy about explaining that the cockatrices had been opposing the dragons for decades, even though the dragons had never done anything to them. He was willing to do a lot to protect his people, including putting himself against the mayor and the chief of police, and Cooper was in awe. He wished there was more he could do, but at the moment, the only useful thing about Cooper was that he was keeping Valerian calm.

Eventually, things calmed down. Bay left, bouncing on his

feet and looking like he was sure he'd win a Pulitzer for this. The police officers tried to stay longer, but since they weren't going to help, Elijah told them to fuck off, albeit not in those terms. He reminded them they were in clan territory, and that was enough to send them running. They probably couldn't stop thinking about the dead cockatrice splattered on the floor upstairs.

Cooper couldn't, either.

They trudged back into the house, and as soon as the door was closed behind them, Elijah slumped against it. He rubbed a hand on his face, then looked around at the people in the entrance. "Get some rest," he ordered.

"We should probably take care of the bodies first," Jerome grumbled. "They're going to start stinking."

Cooper shuddered at his matter-of-fact tone. He never knew what to think of Jerome, but the man was a clan member and apparently knew how to deal with bodies. This was one time Cooper was happy to be dead. It meant he wouldn't be involved in removing the bodies or trying to scrub out the blood from the carpet.

Elijah swore. "We should."

"I'll take charge of that if you don't mind."

"Please, do. I feel I already have enough on my plate and don't have the energy to focus on dead cockatrices." Elijah looked around again. "I honestly don't know how to protect the clan anymore. I'll do my best, but it's clear the chief of police and the mayor are involved, and if they want to, they can create a lot of trouble for the clan while making everything appear legal."

"You'll manage," Leo said, sounding convinced. "You're the alpha for a reason. We have faith in you."

He was talking for everyone in the room, possibly for everyone in the clan. Cooper agreed with him. He trusted Elijah as their alpha, and he knew the dragon shifter would do anything in his power to keep the clan safe.

The problem was that it might not be enough.

# Chapter Ten

Days later, the cleanup was still underway. Valerian doubted there was anything anyone could do to get the blood out of the carpet upstairs, and he'd started to avoid going down that hallway. Elijah had mentioned replacing the carpet outright, and Valerian would stay away until that happened.

He didn't need a reminder of what the cockatrice shifter had said and what he would have done if he'd managed to get his hands on Valerian. Just the thought was enough to make Valerian shudder in horror, and he firmly pushed his thoughts away from the dead cockatrice.

The man would never hurt Valerian. He'd never touch him. Elijah had made sure of that.

Valerian had been helping around the house as much as he could, even though Cooper had insisted he needed rest. He felt back to normal by now, and he was a clan member. He wanted to do his part like everyone else.

Besides, cleaning the house was a good activity because it meant he could think about what had happened with Cooper as he put everything back to rights. Cleaning wasn't something he had to think about as he did it, and it allowed him to focus on how to make Cooper corporeal.

Valerian had succeeded. It hadn't lasted long enough, but Cooper had become corporeal, and he'd used that to defend Valerian and the others. Even Olsen had seen him, which meant Valerian was getting better at it. If that was what he'd managed to do with two psychics touching him, what would happen if all of them did?

He wanted to ask them to try that, but he was afraid. Besides, he was sure Victor would nix the idea until they could research it more thoroughly. If it was up to Valerian, he'd already have tried to make Cooper permanently corporeal at least a dozen times since the attack. When he'd brought it up to Victor, though, Victor had cautioned him against using too much of his power and had warned him to be sure he knew what he was doing before doing anything.

The problem was that Valerian had no idea what he was doing. He'd had no idea what would happen when he'd made Cooper corporeal during the attack. He hadn't expected that having York and Victor touching him would boost Cooper as much as it had, but now he couldn't stop thinking about it. He wanted Cooper back permanently. He wanted more than the kisses between them. He wanted Cooper forever, and right now, he didn't care what it cost him.

Putting down the vacuum, he decided he needed a break. If he happened to take that break with Victor, no one would blame him.

Victor was, as always, in the library. A few cockatrice shifters had managed to get in there, and they'd done a lot of damage. Luckily, most of the books seemed to be intact, but many of them were piled up in the middle of the room as if the cockatrices had been building up a pyre. Valerian wouldn't put that past them, but he didn't want to think about them setting fire to the pyre and the rest of the house.

Victor was re-shelving books, but he smiled at Valerian when he saw him. "I was wondering how long it would take you to grow impatient and come talk to me."

Valerian rolled his eyes. "It didn't take a genius to know I'd come."

"I suppose it didn't. Do you want to do this now?"

Valerian eyed him warily. "Are you going to tell me I

shouldn't make Cooper permanently corporeal?"

"Never. I want you to have this, and as far as I know, there's nothing that forbids it."

"What is it, then?"

Victor sighed and moved toward the small area with the couches and chairs. He sat heavily into one of the chairs, and Valerian sat with him, waiting to see what would happen. He couldn't do this by himself, which meant he had to convince the psychics to lend him their energy, abilities, or whatever he'd used the first time.

Maybe that was the problem and the reason Victor wanted to know more about how this worked before they did anything. Valerian could understand, but that didn't mean he wasn't impatient.

He told himself to give Victor a chance to explain what he was thinking. It was the only way for him to know and the only way for them to talk things out and get over this hurdle.

"I'll be honest," Victor started. "I'm a bit lost when it comes to all of this. I'm a psychic, and I've never seen the kind of power you used in that storage room. That means it probably has to do with your mage side, which means Gunther should be here to talk to you."

The mage hadn't been around since the attack, almost as if he was avoiding the clan. Valerian doubted that, so he took out his phone and quickly dialed Gunther's number. He put the call on speaker and placed his phone on the table, and both he and Victor stared as it rang.

"Is everything all right with the clan?" Gunther asked when he answered.

"Everything's fine," Valerian reassured him. "But Victor and I are talking about what happened in the storage room."

Gunther chuckled. "Let me guess. You were trying to convince him he should allow you to try again, and he's hesitant because he doesn't know how it works or what could happen if it goes wrong."

"That's pretty much it," Victor confirmed. "We agree that Valerian's ability probably belongs more to the mage side of him than it does to the psychic side. It's why I believe you should be here. You're the only mage I know outside Valerian, and I'm hoping you know what's going on and how to deal with it."

"I do agree that what Valerian can do when it comes to ghosts is probably anchored in his mage side. It was interesting to see the way Valerian works. I didn't expect him to be divided into mage and psychic, but the powers mingled and became something entirely different. I might be a mage, but that doesn't mean I know how to deal with this."

Victor sighed. "And you wouldn't happen to know someone who does?"

There was a moment of hesitation. Valerian didn't know how to take it, but he stayed silent and gave Gunther time to think.

"I could contact my mentor," Gunther finally said.

"Doesn't she live with you and your coven?"

"Not anymore, and she hasn't in a long time. I know you're impatient, Valerian, and I understand why. Give me a few days, okay? I wish we could do this right now, but Victor isn't wrong when he says we don't know what will happen or what the results could be if you don't do this properly."

Valerian wanted to say no. He scowled at the phone, even though Gunther couldn't see him. In the end, though, he had to admit that both he and Victor were right.

Valerian would never forgive himself if something were to happen to one of his friends or Cooper. He didn't know how it worked, and he might take too much power from the psychics and hurt both them and Cooper. There was also the fact that they didn't know if Gunther could help, too, or if the mage's power would be different from a psychic's. It could take them years to experiment, but Valerian didn't want to wait years, so it was better to contact someone who knew what they were doing.

"All right. Contact your mentor and see what she says. I'm not waiting forever, though. I want Cooper permanently corporeal, and if no one has any suggestions, I'll just try it and see what happens."

Gunther laughed. "That sounded like a threat."

"I suppose you can consider it one."

"Then you consider this done. I'll contact my mentor and let you know what she says."

Once again, the only thing Valerian could do was wait.


Cooper glared at the dragon shifter tearing out the carpet. It didn't look like fun. If anything, it looked tiring and kind of horrible, considering how much blood had soaked into the carpet.

But at least the dragon shifter was doing something. He didn't look happy about it, but he was making the house clean so it would look like the cockatrices had never been there, which was what Cooper wanted to do, too.

But he couldn't, because he was a ghost.

In the beginning, right after Cooper had died, he'd been confused. He didn't know what had happened, and it had been hard to understand and wrap his mind around. Once he did, he'd been angry. His death wasn't fair, and it still felt that way. He'd made his peace with the fact that he'd died, but it hadn't been easy.

He was angry again. If he weren't dead, he could be helping, and not just with the cleaning. He could have done more to keep Valerian and the others safe.

Besides, this was his home, too. He should be participating in the cleaning like everyone else instead of hanging around spying on the people who were actually doing something.

"Glaring at the guy isn't going to help you or him," Kenneth said from behind Cooper.

Cooper glared at him, too, just for good measure. "I'm aware of that."

"Then you should stop. You don't want your face to be stuck that way, do you?"

The absurd comment made Cooper snort, and he allowed himself to relax.

Kenneth was right. Being angry wouldn't help anyone—not Cooper, not Valerian, not the clan. Cooper needed to stay calm instead of giving in to his emotions.

"I just hate being this useless," he told Kenneth.

"I can understand that. I knew I wouldn't be able to protect my family when the clan was attacked, and it was both terrifying and frustrating. It is what it is, but maybe there *is* something we can do."

Cooper considered Kenneth's words. "Like what?"

"We're ghosts. The cockatrices don't have psychics."

"They have Curt's girlfriend."

"But she's only one person, so we can easily hide from her. No one else will see us, which means they can't hurt us. We can poke around, listen in to conversations, and maybe find out what the cockatrices alpha is planning."

Cooper didn't even hesitate. "Let's go."

Kenneth chuckled, and they both went.

Traveling as a ghost was weird. Obviously, they didn't need to take a car, but they also didn't need to walk all the way there. Cooper just had to focus on where he was going, and after a few moments, he got there.

He'd spent enough time in cockatrice territory to remember it well. It wasn't the first time he and Kenneth were there together, so he wasn't surprised when Kenneth appeared next to him. They'd both been thinking about the house where

Valerian had been kept, and now they stood in front of it.

Cooper's stomach churned as he looked up at it. Valerian had spent too much time here, trapped and in pain. Cooper wanted nothing more than to set it on fire, but he wasn't corporeal, since Valerian wasn't here. That was probably for the best. Cooper wouldn't be surprised if the cockatrices used an accidental fire — or not that accidental, if Cooper was behind it — against the dragons in some way.

"Where do we start?" Kenneth asked.

"I'm not sure. Do we know if the house is empty?"

"There's only one way to find out."

Kenneth and Cooper drifted into the house. Cooper agreed to have Kenneth check upstairs because he never wanted to see that room again. He stayed downstairs, poking around the living room, then the kitchen. It looked like a family home. He'd had time to roam the house while Valerian was still there, but he hadn't done it often. He hadn't wanted to leave Valerian alone for too long, especially when he'd been at his most vulnerable. Luckily, Valerian was safe now. He'd never be hurt again if Cooper had anything to say about it.

While Cooper waited for Kenneth, he glanced at the pictures on the wall. He moved closer when he realized he'd recognized one of the people in them. Terrence looked happier here, more relaxed, and not frightened. He had his arm around a woman's shoulders, while a young boy hung from his neck. The three of them were grinning, and Cooper wondered if this was Terrence's family. If it was, where were they?

"Nothing," Kenneth said, startling Cooper.

"I didn't expect anyone to be here beyond the owners of the house. Where do you think we'll find Curt?"

"Probably the alpha's house. I know where it is."

Cooper nodded and put a hand on Kenneth's shoulder. They'd found out they could travel like this a while ago when they'd talked about what being dead meant to both of them.

Cooper had grown close to Kenneth, which was kind of odd. Kenneth was almost a father figure to him, but he was too young to be Cooper's father, or rather, he'd been too young when he died. Technically, he was old enough to be Cooper's grandfather.

Sometimes being a ghost was complicated.

Cooper didn't know the next house they appeared in front of. He followed Kenneth's lead, and he didn't miss the way Kenneth was more careful here. Curt's girlfriend might be around, and they couldn't risk her seeing them. Cooper remembered her all too well, and he wasn't looking forward to having to deal with her again, so he hoped he wouldn't have to.

"You know, I've always wondered why the cockatrices keep Curt around," Kenneth said as they looked around the house. "I get that they want to have power and get rid of the clan, but Curt seems like a loose cannon."

Cooper agreed. "He's the alpha's cousin," he explained.

Kenneth cocked his head. "Is he?"

"I heard them talk once, back at the house where Valerian was being kept. Curt was pushing for something, but the alpha wasn't happy with him and refused. Curt insisted that he owed it to him because they were family or something like that."

"It certainly explains why the alpha hasn't kicked him out even though most of his plans have gone to shit."

A door slammed, making both of them jump. Cooper's first instinct was to hide, but he and Kenneth stayed where they were. The only voices they could hear belonged to two men, and as long as Curt's girlfriend wasn't there, no one would see them.

"I can't believe you were so stupid," a loud voice said.

The alpha stormed into the living room but didn't get far because Curt grabbed his arm. "What was I supposed to do?

You weren't doing anything about the dragons."

"That's because there's nothing we should be doing about them. Do you want a war?"

The alpha brushed off Curt's hand. Curt didn't seem to care or be offended. "Yes. I want every single dragon dead. They took everything from me, and I'll take everything from them."

"My cockatrices aren't yours to order around," the alpha yelled. "I'm the alpha, not you."

Cooper and Kenneth looked at each other. What they were hearing made a lot of sense, and Cooper wasn't surprised that Curt had taken things into his own hands. He didn't seem to realize how dangerous it was, but Cooper could see the alpha was *pissed*. Maybe Curt thought that being the man's cousin would protect him, but Cooper wasn't too sure about that.

The alpha pointed his finger at Curt's face. "Don't ever do that again," he ordered. "You won't like what happens if you do."

"You can't stop me," Curt snapped back. "I'm on a mission, and I'll win. You'll see. By the time I'm done, you'll be happy, because all the dragons will be gone, and our clan will own this city."

Cooper had suspected that was Curt's plan. He didn't know if Curt would manage to put it into place, but from the look on the alpha's face, Cooper would be surprised if Curt made it out of the situation in one piece.

Cooper hoped he wouldn't.

# CHAPTER ELEVEN

No one had been surprised when Cooper and Kenneth came back from visiting the cockatrices to tell them that Curt was involved in the attack. Valerian had been angry at Cooper for putting himself in danger, and he couldn't stop feeling that way, even though Cooper was already dead. Nothing could happen to him. No one could touch him, not even a psychic. Even if Curt's girlfriend had happened to be there, she wouldn't have been able to do anything to him, or to Kenneth, for that matter. Valerian was the only one who could touch them, but that didn't mean he hadn't been worried.

Besides, who was to say that he was the only one who could do that? Curt's girlfriend was a mage and a psychic, so in theory, she might be able to touch ghosts, just like Valerian. There had to be a reason Curt had needed him to do it even though his girlfriend was right there, but Valerian didn't know that reason. He was unwilling to put anyone in danger, even ghosts.

"As far as we are aware, the police force isn't investigating the cockatrice shifters," the anchorwoman on the TV screen Valerian had been ignoring said. "I'm sure they have their reasons, but I can't think of what those reasons might be." She turned to a man sitting next to her. "Can you?"

The man leaned forward. "I believe that whatever those reasons are, they can be counted in dollars."

"So you're saying you believe the cockatrice clan is paying our chief of police?"

"Either that or they have something on him. Honestly, I don't care what the reason is. The police force isn't doing its job, and it should. They're here to protect us, but they're not."

"Some people say the police are supposed to protect humans, not dragon shifters," the anchorwoman pointed out.

Valerian resisted the urge to growl. She was playing devil's advocate, and he didn't think she believed what she was saying, but it grated. She was trying to get a rise out of the man defending the dragons, and it was working.

Valerian wasn't sure why he was watching this stuff. He'd been keeping an eye on the news since the attack to see how the humans took what had happened and which side they supported, and he'd been relieved to see they were with the dragons. No matter what the police kept saying, these people lived in the city. They might not be shifters, but it didn't mean they weren't aware of the tension between the dragons and the cockatrices. The fact that the dragons had been attacked at home, in their territory, was evidence that the cockatrice shifters had been in the wrong. Besides, they had a reputation.

The police force might be blind to all of this, but most humans weren't. Several of them were now speaking up for dragons, like the man on the screen, and while Valerian wasn't sure how much good it would do, it was something. It was certainly better than having most of the city against them because they were afraid of them.

Not that humans would be wrong to be afraid of dragon shifters. Valerian trusted the clan with his life, but they weren't the only dragon shifters in the country. He had no doubt that some dragon shifters weren't good people, just like he didn't think all cockatrice shifters were assholes. In this case, most of the city seemed to be on the side of the dragons, which was what they needed, because it meant the cockatrices had stopped attacking them. Between that and the fact that the alpha hadn't ordered the attack, Valerian hoped the dragons were safe.

"The cockatrice shifters have always had a reputation," the man on the screen said. "And I think it's deserved."

"You don't believe they had a good reason to do what they did?"

"What good reason? They attacked the dragons in their territory. That's a no-no for shifters. Their territories are sacred, and the cockatrice attacked the dragons in their home. I'm ready to bet it was unprovoked, too. They thought they'd win, but now they might have a war on their hands. The dragons won't take this lying down."

A war might be what Curt wanted, but Valerian hoped that the cockatrice alpha would realize it wasn't in his people's best interest. Of course, he doubted the man cared about anyone but himself, so he might still be stupid enough to go along with this just because he disliked the dragons.

The TV turned off. Valerian blinked and looked around. Victor stood behind the couch, the remote control still aimed at the screen.

"You shouldn't be watching that stuff," he gently scolded.

"I'm just trying to keep an eye on what the humans think about this situation," Valerian explained.

"I understand, but we have work to do."

Valerian huffed, but he hauled himself to his feet. Victor was right. He needed to get better if he wanted to be of any use to the clan when it came to the fight against the cockatrices.

The problem was that he still had no idea what he was dealing with. He'd been trying to work with Gunther, but the other mage couldn't visit often. Every time he did, he looked more worried, and his expression and the way he behaved were enough to tell Valerian that things weren't going well with his coven. Valerian didn't plan to suggest that Gunther leave his coven, because he couldn't understand how important the coven was in a mage's life, but he'd been tempted more than once.

And when Gunther wasn't there, Valerian focused on the psychic abilities he was still learning. From his mother, he'd learned how to pull ghosts to him and push them away, but over time he'd become rusty. That was what he was focusing on at the moment, and of course he was making Kenneth and Cooper corporeal and experimenting on what made it last longer and what made them visible to Olsen and the dragons. It was a trial-and-error way to do things, but it was the only way they knew, and Valerian was relieved to have something to focus on. Otherwise, he'd spend his entire days in front of the TV, which wouldn't do him any good.

He followed Victor to the library, not surprised to see everyone else was already there. Not every psychic in the house trained regularly, mostly because Victor and his brothers already knew what they were doing. York and Lindsey, on the other hand, were still slightly wobbly as psychics. Valerian was relieved that he wasn't the only one still learning, and he sat with an easy smile, ready to focus on his training and whatever Victor would ask of them today.

*

They were deep in conversation after pulling Kenneth to them for the fifth time when someone knocked on the door. Victor got up to open it. Valerian didn't realize something was happening until Victor didn't come back right away. Valerian turned to him only to find him nodding at whoever was on the other side of the door. Valerian sucked in a breath, wondering what disaster had happened this time, and since he didn't think he could face it on his own, he thought of Cooper and pulled.

Cooper appeared after only a few seconds. He looked around the room, then rolled his eyes. "Do you really have to use me when you're training? I was busy."

"*You* were busy?" Kenneth grumbled. "They've been pulling and pushing me away for half an hour. I think it's your turn to be their guinea pig."

"This session is over," Victor declared. "Valerian, I need you to stay here. Everyone else, we'll see you later."

Valerian bit on his lower lip. "What is it this time?" he asked.

But Victor was smiling. "Gunther is here, and he's not alone."

Valerian didn't want to hope, but he found that he couldn't help it. "Who's with him?"

"His mentor. They're here for you and Cooper."

This time, Valerian couldn't stop himself from hoping.


Cooper watched as Gunther came into the room, followed by an older woman. She appeared in her fifties, with a gentle smile that told Cooper she was there to help. He wanted this as much as Valerian, but he'd been afraid Valerian would be disappointed if they ever found out it wasn't possible. Gunther thought his mentor could help, though, and Cooper wanted to believe him. He wanted to believe that this woman had enough power to help Valerian learn how to deal with what he could do and learn to be better at it.

They didn't know what this ability would mean to Valerian or Cooper. They also still didn't know what else Valerian could do. As far as Cooper was concerned, even if the answer to that question was nothing, he wouldn't care. He wouldn't even care if Valerian couldn't make him permanently corporeal. He just wanted to be with Valerian, and he was. It wasn't always easy when most of the people around them couldn't see Cooper, but if they stayed with the clan, it wouldn't be too bad. There were a lot of psychics here, and the dragons knew that Cooper was around.

But that didn't mean Cooper didn't want to be corporeal.

He hovered close to Valerian as Gunther and the woman settled into a couple of the chairs recently vacated by the psychics. York had wanted to stay, but Cooper had convinced him to go. He'd promised he'd let York know what was happening as soon as he had more information, and thankfully, York had allowed Victor to lead him out. He was probably trying to find Leo right now to tell him what was going on. That meant Cooper and Valerian would have two people to reassure later, but that was all right.

The woman was looking around, taking in the library. Her gaze eventually stopped on Valerian. Cooper inched closer but resisted the urge to touch Valerian in case he didn't want it.

"It's a pleasure to meet you," she said, her voice as warm as her smile. "My name is Amelia, and I was Gunther's mentor and teacher."

"You're not anymore?" Valerian asked.

"He no longer needs me."

Gunther chuckled. "I'll always need you."

Amelia stared at him for a moment. "I suspect that's true. We need to talk once this is over."

Gunther didn't look happy. "There's no reason for you to worry. I'm handling things."

"You shouldn't have to." Amelia peered back at Valerian. "Now, Gunther explained what you're trying to do. Is your ghost here?"

Valerian looked up at Cooper. That was sufficient to let Amelia know where Cooper was, but Cooper still took Valerian's hand, then leaned over to touch the back of her hand.

She didn't jerk away like most people would have. She was a mage, not a psychic, which meant that she couldn't see him. Yet, she didn't seem afraid that someone she couldn't see had touched her.

"That's incredible," she said. "I've heard of this happening but never seen it myself. I take it that was Cooper?"

"It was," Valerian confirmed. "He's touching my hand, which is why you can feel him."

"But I couldn't see him."

"That's only happened that one time in the storage room."

Amelia glanced at Gunther

Gunther nodded. "I already told you what happened back then. But as a quick recap, two other psychics were touching Valerian. One of them was Cooper's brother, although I don't think that who he was matters."

Amelia had a thoughtful expression. "I don't know. Maybe his being one of the psychics who powered Valerian enough to make Cooper corporeal and visible is what made it possible. Cooper's brother would have desperately wanted his brother to materialize, right?"

That much was true. Cooper wished he could be part of the conversation, but with Amelia and Gunther not being able to see or hear him, it was useless for him to try to talk. Besides, he wasn't sure there was anything he could do to help. He didn't know how Valerian's powers worked, and he didn't know how to make them stronger. That was Gunther and Amelia's job, and Cooper was happy to take a step back and let them take the lead.

"That certainly is a possibility," Gunther agreed. "Valerian, have you and the others tried to do this again since the attack?"

"We didn't dare." Valerian wrinkled his nose. "I wanted to try, but Victor convinced me to wait at the very least until you were around. He knows how to handle my psychic abilities but has no idea how to deal with the mage stuff. He didn't want to do this in case something happened."

Amelia didn't look surprised. "He sounds like a good teacher. Maybe we should have him at this meeting."

"I'll text him," Gunther said, taking out his phone.

The door opened, and someone shoved Victor through it. He turned to glare, but the door slammed close again before he could say anything.

He looked at the group around Valerian with a sheepish expression. "Sorry about that," he said as he rubbed the back of his neck. "We were just hanging around waiting for the meeting to be over. We want to be there for Valerian and Cooper."

Amelia laughed. "That's fine. Why don't you get everyone back inside? If you want to give this a try, we'll need other psychics."

The door opened before anyone in the room could do or say anything. York was the first one in, and he avoided looking at Cooper. Cooper wasn't surprised, since he'd asked York to leave and York hadn't listened, but he wasn't angry. If their roles were reversed, he wouldn't have left, either.

Everyone was present, including Olsen. Victor introduced all of them to Amelia. Amelia seemed curious about his presence, but he just shrugged.

"I suppose I'll have time to get to know all of you later," she said. "But it's good to see so many people supporting this. Now, from what I understand, Valerian has the ability to make ghosts corporeal, hopefully permanently. It's not something I've seen, but I've heard of it and already contacted several people who can tell me more. As soon as Gunther told me about this, I knew I wanted to be involved and to help."

"That's all we want," Valerian whispered.

Amelia nodded. "I understand. I'll help you, but I need you to wrap your mind around the fact that even if you manage to do this, you won't bring Cooper back to life. He's dead, and nothing can change that. It also means that you don't know what will happen when you make him corporeal. He might not feel pain or anything at all." Amelia hesitated. "That includes not feeling anything he touches in any circumstance, including intimate ones."

Olsen barked out a laugh. "Are you saying Cooper may not be able to have sex with Valerian?"

"I was trying to be delicate about it, but yes. As I said, I've never seen this done. I can't make any promises, and I have no idea what will happen. I can tell you that I'll be here to help and do everything I can to make sure you and Cooper have what you need."

Valerian looked at Cooper. Cooper wanted Valerian — of course he did. He'd never wanted anyone more, and the thought of not being able to feel him didn't make Cooper happy. If he did this, though, he and Valerian would be together. In the end, that was all that mattered. Cooper didn't care about sex. He hadn't had sex since he died and was perfectly fine.

"I want this," he told Valerian.

"I want it, too." Valerian looked at Amelia. "We're in, whatever it means."

Amelia didn't look surprised. "All right. From what I was told, Valerian has the ability but not the power. A mage's power grows over time as they learn and age, as I'm sure a psychic's power does."

"We get more powerful in time," Victor confirmed. "And it's good to know that the same goes for mages, although I have to admit I'm a little scared of what Valerian might be able to do in ten or twenty years. He's already powerful now."

"I don't think that's true," Valerian argued. "I needed you to rescue me from the cockatrice shifters. I was never able to stand up to my coven. How can you say I'm powerful?"

"You are," Amelia said. "You were never taught how to deal with your powers and abilities, how to have them under control and use them to your benefit, but that can change. I haven't been a mentor in a while, but even before Gunther, I taught several other mages. I can do the same for you, Valerian."

Valerian stared at her as if he couldn't quite believe it. "You want to teach me?"

"If you'll let me."

Valerian didn't hesitate. "I will, but not now. We need to focus on Cooper first."

Amelia nodded. "Then that's what we'll do."


Valerian couldn't believe this was happening. He didn't think he'd make Cooper corporeal today, but they were on the right path, and that was all that mattered.

"So Valerian used Victor and York as batteries," Olsen said after a moment of silence.

Olsen was always eager to participate, even though he wasn't a psychic. Valerian didn't understand it, but he didn't have to. He couldn't understand Olsen, who'd grown up as the only entirely human person in a psychic family yet wasn't bitter.

Amelia nodded. "Mages and psychics aren't the same, of course, but our powers are similar. We all draw from the same source. It means that mages and psychics are compatible. If our powers weren't, Valerian wouldn't be here."

Because he never would have been born. He'd never really thought about these things. He'd been more focused on surviving and running from the coven, but now he didn't have to do that anymore. He was free to study, have friends, a family, and do what he wanted with his life.

"What about dragons?" York asked. His cheeks flushed when everyone turned to him, but he pushed on. "I have no idea how shifters can shift, but to me, it sounds like magic. Is it the same magic that psychics and mages use?"

"That's a good question," Amelia said with a proud smile.

York's cheeks flushed even darker. "Thank you. What I want to know is what would happen if Valerian were to draw power from a dragon, like, for example, my boyfriend. He can turn into a dragon, which has to mean he has much more magic and power than me, right?"

"But why would he do that?" Cooper asked. He looked slightly bewildered. "I mean, I understand he'd do it for you, but me? We have no idea what might happen to him or any other dragon who tries to help that way, and I'm not ready to sacrifice anyone just to become corporeal again."

"I think Gunther and I are missing part of the conversation," Amelia said.

"I apologize. Cooper doesn't understand why Leo would agree to do this." Valerian knew where Cooper was coming from, but even he understood why Leo would want to do this, and it wasn't just because of York.

He turned to look up at Cooper. "Don't you know? You're a clan member, and clan members help each other. I'm sure Leo would do this for York, but that's not the only reason. I think that if you ask any dragon in the clan, they'll volunteer."

Cooper's eyes were wide. "I'm nothing to them. They can't even see me."

"But they know you're here and that you're a clan member. They know how important you are to me." And Valerian was pretty sure that would be reason enough for most of the dragons to help. They wanted him and Cooper to be happy, and that was how they'd obtain that.

"I'm honestly not sure about this," Amelia said. "I'll have to call a few people and send a few more emails, but I'm not making any promises. This is something not many people have done. Mages and psychics seldom meet and mix, let alone have children. I'm afraid to say that the mage's coven often steps in when that happens. We're not the most welcoming of people, and many mages refuse to see anything beyond tradition. They don't want the world to change. They don't want their covens to change."

"I'm aware of that," Valerian grumbled.

"Gunther mentioned something about your coven hunting you."

"They were never my coven. My father belonged with them before he met my mother, but they refused to welcome her, and he left. When they found out about me, they started hunting us. We resisted for fifteen years." Valerian didn't want to talk about this again, so he shook his head. "I just know how covens can be. I don't want you and Gunther to be in trouble."

"I won't be, since I'm not part of any coven anymore," Amelia said. She looked at Gunther. "And I'm thriving. You would be, too, if you let the coven go, especially after what they've been doing."

"What happened?"

Valerian didn't want Gunther to be in trouble because of him, but Gunther didn't explain. Instead, he glared at Amelia, then looked at Valerian.

"It would certainly help if a dragon could power you. Considering how big they are and how much magic it takes for them to shift, one should be enough for you to do this. It might be too much, though, which is why I'd wait to try until we have more information, especially on the kind of magic shifters have."

Valerian didn't want to wait any longer, but he couldn't deny Gunther was right. What would happen if he used his magic and made Leo explode or something? Valerian wasn't willing to risk anyone's life, not even his own. Cooper was more important to him than anyone else had ever been, but they'd talked about this and agreed. They'd only do this if it was safe for everyone involved. If it wasn't, they'd wait and try to find another way. They weren't giving up. They were just being careful.

"I want to be involved," Valerian said. "I understand we need to research, and I want to be part of it. You're all working hard for Cooper and me. I don't know if we'll ever be able to thank you enough for what you're doing, even if we never manage to make Cooper corporeal. It's only right that I take on some of the work."

Gunther grinned. "I don't see any problem with that. Unfortunately, most of what I need to do is talk to people I know. You could go over some books for me, though."

"I'll do anything." Valerian looked around. "You think we can find answers in here?"

"I don't know about these books, but I can think of a few in the coven's library."

"If you do this, the coven won't be happy," Amelia warned.

Gunther glared at her. "I'm aware. Do you or do you not want me to leave the coven?"

"And you're doing so by stealing books?"

"I'm doing so by helping my friends."

Amelia stared at him for a moment. Then she nodded. Obviously, she cared about Gunther and wanted him to leave the coven, and even though Valerian didn't know what was going on there, he had to agree. Gunther hadn't been spending a lot of time with them. Valerian didn't think he was happy about that, and when he *was* around, he always looked tired and a bit angry. If that was what being with his coven did, then maybe it would be better for him not to be with them.

But it wasn't Valerian's place to say anything about that. Gunther already knew he'd always be welcome with the clan and that the dragons would protect him even if he didn't want to become a clan member. Valerian had been watching the clan since he'd arrived, so he knew how important Gunther was to Elijah. He hadn't asked because it was none of his business, but he was pretty sure Elijah would do anything for Gunther.

"Let's focus on this," Gunther said. "We can think about the coven later. As it is, the less I think about them, the better I feel." He looked at Valerian. "Why don't we try doing this with Victor and York touching you like last time? That way, Amelia can see how it works and have more details to give her friends when she explains what's happening."

Valerian sighed. He'd known he'd have to work hard today, and if it was for Cooper, he was ready to do it. That didn't mean he had to be happy about it or that it would be fun.

He gestured at Victor and York to approach him. It was time to get to work.


Cooper and Valerian were growing closer quickly now that Valerian was safe. Cooper still had trouble believing they could really do this and that he'd be corporeal again soon. He understood why Amelia had tried cautioning him and Valerian, but he couldn't *not* hope.

Valerian had done it once, during the attack. He could do it again, and if he succeeded, it would be permanent. Cooper would truly be part of Valerian's life. He could stand by his side and with their friends as they faced the danger the cockatrices represented. He could help protect the clan, which was all he'd wanted since he'd become a member.

But not right now. It would take a little time to happen, and Cooper would need patience. Good thing he had as much time as Valerian would need, since he was dead.

"You should get some rest," he told Valerian. If he didn't push Valerian to rest, Valerian would work until he was exhausted, no matter what Gunther and Amelia said.

Valerian looked like he was about to protest, so Cooper

arched a brow. He could be convincing when he wanted to be. Pushing Valerian to do anything would be useless because he'd dig in his heels.

Valerian's cheeks flushed. "I do feel tired."

Cooper snickered, ignored the other psychics watching them—especially his brother—and grabbed Valerian's hand. He pulled him away, ignoring Valerian's yelp, and waved at the people in the room. Not everyone could see them, but the ones who could were explaining what was happening. Cooper didn't care. He needed time with Valerian and didn't care what everyone else thought of that.

"Did you have to be so obvious?" Valerian grumbled.

"Everyone knows we're together, Val."

"Val?"

Cooper turned and grinned back. "You don't like it?"

"I like it just fine."

From the way his cheeks were still flushed, Cooper thought it was true.

"But even though they know about us, they don't have to know what we're going to do."

"And what are we going to do?" Cooper teased.

Valerian's cheeks were on fire now. "You know."

Cooper did know. He'd been waiting a long time for this. He hadn't dared hope he and Valerian would ever have this, but they did. Even if Valerian was never able to make Cooper permanently corporeal, they would always be together. It was time to stop waiting for the right moment, for when the cockatrices wouldn't be a danger anymore, for when Cooper would be corporeal again. The right time was now or whenever they were ready for it.

But Cooper needed to be sure Valerian was on board with this, so he slowed down once they reached Valerian's bedroom. He watched as Valerian sat on the edge of his mattress, then he joined him.

"What do you want?" he whispered, taking one of Valerian's hands.

Valerian kept his focus on the floor, but Cooper wasn't offended. He knew his guy, so he was aware that it was easier for Valerian to talk and be honest if he didn't have to look at him.

"So many things that I don't know where to start," Valerian said.

"I'll give you anything you want."

"I know. And I know you won't leave me. I have faith in you and in us."

"So do I. No matter what happens next, whatever you manage or don't manage to do with your abilities, I'm not going anywhere."

Valerian looked up. "That's all I need to know. And I do want this, Cooper, but you know what my life before was like. I never had the time to think about love or even sex. I was always on the run, always hiding from the coven."

It took Cooper a moment to understand what Valerian was saying. He wasn't surprised when he did. "You've never been with anyone."

"I haven't. And I don't care that I don't have that experience. I like that you'll be the first because I love you."

Valerian's cheeks were flaming, and he was looking everywhere but at Cooper, but that was all right. "I love you, too. I'll take care of you, whatever happens."

"I know."

Cooper groaned and reached for Valerian. Valerian easily came when Cooper pulled him onto his lap, still amazed at the fact that they could touch as if Cooper were alive. He could feel Valerian, and Valerian could feel him.

He cupped Valerian's face with both his hands and kissed him. Valerian didn't hesitate to kiss him back. He was more assertive now that he was safe and sure of Cooper's feelings, and he clung to him, letting him know what he wanted without words. Cooper reached between them, eager to touch skin. Everything else faded—there were no cockatrices, no Curt, no one who could hurt them. There was only them.

Forever.

Cooper hauled Valerian up. Valerian squeaked, but Cooper didn't give him the time to worry. He twisted and dropped him on the bed, then pulled down the jeans he'd opened. He got them to Valerian's knees before giving up and lurching forward.

Valerian jerked when Cooper swallowed his cock. He looked down with wide eyes, but Cooper was focused on what he was doing. He wanted to give Valerian pleasure, to show him one more thing he could give him. This was the closest two people could be, and Valerian had chosen Cooper. Cooper would never forget that, and he'd do everything in his power to make Valerian happy.

Cooper wrapped his lips around Valerian's cock and sucked hard. Valerian groaned, pushing Cooper to do more, to give him everything.

"You can feel me," Valerian murmured reverently.

Cooper had to let go to answer. "Always. Whatever happens, we'll deal with it together."

Valerian nodded. "Yes."

Cooper leaned over him again and took him into his mouth. Valerian's body tensed, but he didn't push Cooper away. He wanted this as much as Cooper did.

Valerian arched his back, pushing deeper into Cooper's mouth as he tangled his fingers in the comforter he was lying on. His moans filled the room, spurning Cooper to push him further. He wanted Valerian to come on his tongue, to take his taste inside of him, and to carry a part of him in his body even when they weren't touching anymore and he wasn't corporeal.

Cooper twirled his tongue around the head of Valerian's cock, then ran it along the length before coming back up. He dedicated some time to the head, sucking gently before dipping his tongue into the slit. Valerian's taste made Cooper moan. He wanted more. He *needed* more.

He cupped Valerian's balls and rolled them between his fingers, gently tugging on them to drive Valerian to the edge. He could tell it wouldn't take long when Valerian's cock jerked against his tongue. Cooper felt lightheaded, but he didn't need to breathe. He was dead. The only thing he needed was Valerian, and he had him in his arms.

Valerian jerked and grabbed Cooper's hair to try to push him away, but Cooper wasn't going anywhere. He caught Valerian under his ass and pulled him closer just as Valerian's cock twitched and spurted against his tongue. It took a bit of fumbling, but Cooper swallowed, holding Valerian until he felt him relax again. Then, he let him down, but he didn't go far. He never wanted to.

He rolled to his side and settled next to Valerian. He was staring at the ceiling, and for a moment, Cooper wondered if something was wrong. "Val? Did I hurt you?"

Valerian shook his head but didn't look at Cooper, which didn't reassure him.

"Valerian? Please talk to me."

Valerian rolled his head to finally look at Cooper. "I'm fine."

"You don't look fine."

"I am. It was just a lot."

It had been the first time someone had done that to Valerian, so it made sense that he was overwhelmed. Cooper was reassured, and he pulled Valerian closer. Valerian cuddled against him, only to freeze seconds later.

"You didn't come," he said, pushing up on an elbow.

"I don't need to."

"That doesn't sound right."

Cooper smiled. "Maybe not, but I really don't. I just want you in my arm, and I have you. Besides, we can do it again later, yeah?"

Valerian's cheeks flushed, but he leaned back down only to pop back up again. Cooper huffed, but he was amused.

"What?" Valerian grumbled. "My jeans are uncomfortable."

Cooper laughed and pulled Valerian down. "Get comfortable, then. I'm not done with you."

If Cooper had things his way, he never would be. Whatever happened or didn't happen next, they'd face it together.

# Chapter Twelve

"Oh, come on. We've already watched this dozens of times," Roslin complained.

"It's a classic," Olsen told him.

"It's not a classic. It's a bad eighties movie."

Olsen gasped. "How dare you. Have you *seen* Kevin Bacon in this movie?"

"I've also seen the badly made giant snakes."

"They're not snakes. They're worms."

Valerian tuned out the brothers. He didn't care what they watched, mostly because he was sure he'd fall asleep halfway through the movie. He'd never felt so safe here in Cooper's arms, cuddling in the corner of the couch. Dinner had been great, and he'd eaten too much. His lids felt heavy, and he should have gone to bed, but he wanted more time with his friends and family.

Even though Roslin and Olsen were bickering like children.

Olsen held up the remote control. "I'm putting it on," he declared.

"I'm sure you can find another Kevin Bacon movie," Roslin protested.

The remote control flew from Olsen's fingers. They both stared at it, and they weren't the only ones. Valerian had no idea what had happened until he saw the ghosts.

Then he understood.

A dozen ghosts appeared, coming in through the walls. Olsen couldn't see them, so he didn't react, but Roslin squeaked and took a step back. The ghosts picked up whatever they could get their hands on, throwing it at the walls and the people in the living room. Olsen couldn't ignore that and rushed to hide behind one of the couches.

"What's going on?" he yelled.

Valerian and Cooper looked at each other. Valerian had no idea what was happening, but he could take a wild guess. Curt was probably involved, and Valerian wouldn't let him hurt his friends.

He got to his feet. Thankfully, the noise was bringing more people to the living room, and a lot of the psychics had already been there. It meant they could take charge right away, hopefully before the ghosts managed to destroy half the house.

"Psychics," Victor's voice came strong as he walked into the living room. "You know what to do."

Valerian's heart raced. He'd never really done this with anyone who wasn't a friend. While he'd been on the run, he hadn't needed to push away ghosts, and here, during his training, he'd only done so with Cooper and Kenneth. There was no way to know how these ghosts would react to him pushing them away, but that wasn't going to stop him.

"I'm here," Cooper said, pressing a hand against Valerian's back.

"I know." It was all Valerian needed. He closed his eyes and focused on the energy he could feel in the room.

In the beginning, he hadn't known what to look for, but Victor was a great teacher. Valerian could feel the difference between a living body and a dead ghost, so it wasn't hard for him to home in on to one of the ghosts. He gathered his energy and pushed.

The ghosts shrieked. Valerian resisted the urge to cover his ears, because he didn't want to break his concentration. He continued pushing, and eventually, the force pushing back vanished. He blinked his eyes open only to jerk back as one of the other ghosts launched herself at him. Her mouth was open on a scream Valerian couldn't hear, and he was grateful for that.

Her fingers were like claws, and she raked them down Valerian's cheek. It burned, and this was the one moment in which he hated being able to make ghosts corporeal. She wouldn't have been able to touch him otherwise, and she seemed to understand something was happening, because she reached for him again.

Cooper placed himself between the two. He caught her wrist, then pushed her back, making her stumble.

"Send her away," Cooper ordered without looking away from her.

Valerian licked his lips and nodded, then focused again.

Once the woman was gone, he looked around the room. He wasn't the only one sporting scratches. These ghosts were stronger than usual, and there was no doubt in his mind that Curt was involved. Maybe his girlfriend had enough power to make the ghosts slightly corporeal, or maybe Curt had found another way to make this work. Whatever the reason behind the scratches on everyone's faces and hands, Valerian was furious.

They were supposed to be safe in this house, dammit. Valerian wasn't sure what Curt was trying to obtain, but this wouldn't do more than annoy them. It certainly wouldn't scare them.

With so many psychics, the room was empty of ghosts after only a few minutes. The only one who remained was Cooper, who came to stand next to him. Valerian leaned against him, needing to reassure himself they were both okay.

"I guess that was a way to spend a Friday night," Olsen said, peeking out from behind the couch. When he saw no one else was moving, he got to his feet. "Can anyone tell me what happened?"

"A bunch of ghosts came in. We sent them away, but they still managed to do some damage." Valerian looked around and winced.

All the art that had been on the walls was on the floor now, the frames broken and pieces of glass everywhere. The vases and plants were in the same state, and Valerian was pretty sure that everyone in the room except maybe Olsen was bleeding from scratches. Even the few dragon shifters who'd been here, like Leo, were bleeding.

A loud screech made all of them jump. The ghost of a tall man with broad shoulders came in through the wall, aimed right at Valerian. Valerian reacted instinctively. Cooper's arms were still around him, so Valerian grabbed the person closest to him and was hit with a wall of power. Without thinking, he channeled that power into pushing away the ghost. The ghost froze, his eyes wide and his mouth open. Valerian only intended to push him away like he had with the others, but instead, this ghost *exploded.*

Valerian stared, unable to comprehend what he'd done. Pieces of the ghost were still drifting to the floor, disappearing before they hit. Eventually, there was nothing left of the man, and Valerian let go of the hand he'd grabbed as if it had burned him. When he looked, he realized he'd grabbed Leo — a dragon shifter.

"Can anyone tell me what happened again?" Olsen whined. "I hate not being able to see."

Victor cleared his throat. "Another ghost came in. I think he startled Valerian, because Valerian grabbed onto Leo and channeled his magic. The ghost didn't just vanish or get pushed away. It exploded."

Olsen gaped at Valerian. "Seriously? You made a ghost explode?"

Valerian didn't know how to answer. It *was* him, but he had no idea how he'd done it. He hadn't even known it was possible before it happened.

The sound of something falling in the hallway made all of them jump. Victor rushed through the door, everyone behind him. Valerian went along in case they needed his help, only to stumble back at the sight in front of him.

Curt.

He was running away from them. There was a window open at the end of the hallway, clearly the way he'd come in, and he was headed straight toward it.

Cooper grabbed one of Valerian's hands, and this time, when Valerian touched Leo, there was intent. He and Leo looked at each other, and when Leo nodded, Valerian focused. He only needed to make Cooper corporeal for a moment.

That would be more than enough for him to get rid of Curt.


Cooper could feel the power flowing into him. He didn't know why Valerian was doing this, but he had a good idea, so he took everything Valerian was willing to give him. It felt different—like the time in the storage room, but even more powerful. Cooper was slightly worried about Valerian over-extending himself, but he had other things to focus on right now.

Like Curt, who had reached the open window and was trying to climb through it.

"Go," Valerian ordered.

His voice was strong, and he was surrounded by people who cared about him, so Cooper wasn't too worried. He and several others ran after Curt, and the way Curt's eyes widened and he paled when he saw them was almost comical. What would be even more comical was Cooper punching him in the face, so Cooper ran faster, ignoring the gasps around him. Valerian had made him corporeal, so he was probably also visible to the people who normally wouldn't see him.

But Cooper got there too late. Curt's foot slid off the window just as Cooper reached it, and he swore as he slammed his hand against the wall. "Dammit."

"Go through," someone said, and Cooper hurried to obey.

They were on the ground floor, but even not, he was a dead man. He couldn't die again.

He scrambled out the window. The gate had been repaired, and while the press had eventually gotten bored and left, a few stragglers were camping outside, hoping for a peek at a fight. The commotion clearly alerted them that something was happening. One of the men raised his camera to snap pictures, and Cooper briefly wondered if he'd be visible in the pictures. Would it look like Curt was running from no one and nothing? Or would Cooper be right there for everyone to see? He didn't have anyone who would be stunned at finding out he was still alive. The only person in his life before the clan was York, and he was here and knew what was happening with Cooper. Cooper didn't care about who found out about him. He just cared about stopping Curt.

He finally reached him and grabbed his arm. Curt stumbled and started falling forward, and Cooper could already taste the victory of pinning him to the ground and forcing him to pay for what he'd done to Valerian. He should have remembered that Curt was a shifter, but he didn't until he felt Curt's skin ripple under his fingertips.

One of the photographers outside the gate cried out. Cooper stumbled back, unwilling to be close to Curt as he shifted into a cockatrice. They might not be as large as dragons, but that didn't mean they weren't lethal. They had wings and claws, and Cooper had no doubt Curt wouldn't hesitate to kill him if he could.

Or he'd try to, anyway.

But he didn't. Cooper could hear people yelling and running toward him and Curt, so he had a pretty good idea why that was. Curt only fought when he knew he'd win. In this case, it was obvious he wouldn't. Cooper wasn't alone. He had his entire clan behind him, ready to take him on in a fight.

Obviously, Curt knew that. He opened his wings and rushed toward the gate. He started rising into the air but couldn't get the height he needed fast enough. His lower legs slammed against the gate, making Cooper wince as the gates flew open. The journalists outside of the gate rushed in, and Cooper moved back. Curt was gone, anyway. It would be of no use to continue running after him, and at the moment, the clan was in another kind of danger.

"Can you tell us who that was?" one of the journalists asked, her phone raised to Cooper's face.

He almost batted her hand away, but he didn't dare. He wasn't entirely sure he was still corporeal, but since they were talking to him, he knew he was at least visible to people who weren't psychics. He didn't know for how much longer, but even though the power Cooper had felt this time around was much stronger than the other times, he didn't dare believe it was permanent. He could easily soon vanish from sight again, and he didn't want that to happen in front of the people filming and snapping pictures.

"That was a cockatrice shifter," another journalist said. "Can you give us their name? Why were they here?"

"Have they attacked again?

"What will your alpha do about it? Is war about to start between the dragons and cockatrices?"

Cooper shook his head and tried to leave, but the journalists pushed ahead. They didn't seem to care that they were invading private property. They wanted their answers.

"Enough!" a strong voice said.

Cooper could have kissed Elijah. The journalists stopped

moving, and Cooper took advantage of it. He quickly walked away, joining the group that was watching the scene from closer to the house. The only one who stepped forward was Elijah, who was pushing his way through the crowd so he could face the journalists.

"You're in dragon territory," he said in a booming voice. "And you are uninvited."

"We apologize," the first woman said, but she seemed to be the only smart person in the group.

"Can you tell us more about what happened just now?" one of the men asked.

"You need to leave." Elijah wasn't shy about dealing with the journalists. "The clan already has agreed to give someone the exclusive over what happens with the cockatrice shifters, and none of you are that person. You're also invading our territory, and I'm ready to call the police if you don't step out."

One of the men snorted and mumbled something that sounded like, "As if they'd do anything."

He was lucky Elijah wasn't a bad person. As it was, Elijah's eyes flashed with anger, and he took a step toward the man. That was enough to send the journalists back, even though Elijah was still in his human form and would never hurt any of them. He was only trying to defend his people and his clan. Surely, the journalists could see that.

"I hope the gate isn't broken again," Leo mumbled as he made his way toward Elijah to help him close it.

Cooper rushed to Valerian's side, taking one of his hands and pulling him toward the house. "What are you doing?" Valerian asked.

Cooper didn't stop until they were inside, shielded from everyone's gaze. Then he pushed Valerian against the wall and kissed him. Valerian squeaked, but he didn't push Cooper away. Instead, he wrapped his arms around him and clung to him, almost as if he was afraid to lose him.

He never would. Even if Cooper remained a ghost and was never permanently corporeal, Valerian would always be able to touch him like this. In the end, that was all that mattered. Cooper wanted to be corporeal because it would make everyone's life easier, but he didn't need it as long as he had Valerian by his side.

"You were incredible," he murmured against Valerian's lips.

"I didn't do anything."

"You did. I felt it, and the journalists could see me." Cooper grimaced as he pressed their foreheads together. "I wish they hadn't, but it doesn't matter. Elijah is taking care of that situation."

Valerian sighed. "What about Curt?"

"I'm pretty sure we lost him."

Cooper didn't know whether one of the dragon shifters had shifted and gone after Curt, but even if they had, it wasn't like they could catch him midair. The city's human population would freak out, which wasn't what anyone wanted.

The dragons wanted to be left to live their lives in peace, and so did Cooper. He didn't fully understand why the cockatrice shifters wanted the dragons dead as much as they did, but he didn't care. The clan hadn't done anything to them. They were in the wrong here, and the dragons would defend themselves if they attacked again. Hopefully, Curt had finally learned his lesson, although Cooper wasn't entirely sure about that. Maybe it was time for the cockatrice alpha to deal with his cousin. Whatever he did, Cooper didn't care as long as Curt stayed away from the clan and the people he loved.

A door opened, but Cooper didn't push away from Valerian. He didn't have a reason to because everyone knew they were together.

And that was what mattered. He and Valerian, the clan, and making sure the cockatrices didn't hurt the dragons ever again.

Valerian was stunned by what he'd managed to do. He hadn't been sure it would work, but after he'd been able to make that ghost explode, he'd been hopeful. Cooper was corporeal and visible to everyone, and even though he hadn't caught Curt, it didn't matter. The only thing that did was that Valerian had done it. He'd made Cooper corporeal, and he felt almost alive against Valerian.

Valerian doubted it would last for much longer. He hadn't used enough power, mostly because he hadn't had time. He also hadn't wanted to draw too much from Leo when they didn't know what might happen to him or Cooper. They would have to experiment, see how long things lasted and how much Valerian could take, but for now, he was pretty sure Cooper wouldn't be corporeal for much longer. Valerian wanted to take advantage of it, but they couldn't.

Their friends streamed in through the door, all of them talking excitedly. Elijah wasn't there, but then, he was probably making sure the journalists wouldn't come in again and that the gate was closed.

York cried out when he saw Cooper and rushed toward him. He hesitated before touching him, but Cooper stepped away from Valerian and easily pulled his brother into his arms. Valerian was pretty sure he heard York sob.

It wasn't the first time the brothers hugged since Cooper's death, but Cooper had always needed to be touching Valerian. It had been slightly awkward, and that meant he and York didn't have as much privacy as they deserved. They could right now, so Valerian moved toward the group to give them space.

Leo was watching him with wide eyes. "I had no idea it was going to be like that," he said.

"You took power from Leo?" Victor asked. "I thought that was what happened, but I wasn't sure."

"I did. I hoped Cooper would catch up to Curt, but unfortunately, he didn't."

"I don't think it matters. What does matter is what you just did."

Valerian shuffled his feet. Victor had told him they needed to wait and experiment, yet Valerian had used Leo's power after barely asking him if it was okay. Leo had nodded, but they should have talked about it. "I'm sorry," Valerian whispered.

Victor squeezed Valerian's shoulder. "I know what I said about experimenting and being careful, but you did what you could in an emergency. This means that you can do it, Valerian. You drew enough power from Leo to make Cooper corporeal, and he still is. You can bring him back by using a mix of your ability and a dragon's magic."

Valerian found himself smiling. He *had* done it, hadn't he? It wouldn't be permanent, but that was only because he'd taken such a small amount of power from Leo. Once they understood how much was needed to make it permanent, Valerian would do it, and Cooper would never be a ghost again. They could be together, and Cooper would be a true member of the clan.

Valerian didn't fool himself into thinking that everything would be roses and butterflies. Life was hard, even without the challenge of being dead. But they'd work things out together. They weren't facing these challenges alone. The clan would help in any way they could, like they already had. Whatever happened next, the clan would face it as a team.

And Valerian and Cooper would face it as a couple.

# CHAPTER THIRTEEN

Valerian was ready to do this. He'd slept a full twelve hours last night after transferring power from Leo to Cooper and making Cooper corporeal for several hours. It had given them the time to experiment a bit and find out what Cooper's body would be able to do and feel. From what they'd found out, Cooper didn't feel pain, and he didn't bleed. When he was hurt, his body healed without him even noticing. He could feel pleasure, though, including arousal.

Valerian's cheeks flushed at the memories of how he and Cooper had tested that.

"You're adorable when you blush," Cooper said from the other side of the bed.

Valerian turned to face him, pulling the sheet up until it reached his chin. He looked at Cooper, who was in his usual place waiting for Valerian to wake up.

Right now, he wasn't visible to anyone but psychics. It had lasted for hours, but after he and Valerian had made love, Cooper had gone downstairs. He'd confirmed that the dragons couldn't see him anymore. He'd found out because a dragon had screamed at the sight of a plate and a glass walking down the hallway on their own. Cooper had been the one carrying them, but the dragon hadn't been able to see him.

But that was okay. Valerian had already decided that today was the day, and he wouldn't let anyone change his mind. He understood why Victor was cautious, but he was done waiting.

He'd texted Gunther and Amelia last night to tell them

what had happened and what he was planning. They'd both promised they'd be here today, and Valerian hoped they would. He wanted them to be present in case something bad happened, but he was trying not to focus on that. He didn't want to do this while thinking he might hurt someone, especially someone who was volunteering to help. He just had to keep in mind that he'd done it once already and that if the magic of one dragon wasn't enough, he had plenty of volunteers. Hell, even Jerome had offered his magic, which had stunned Valerian.

"But then, you're always adorable," Cooper murmured as he leaned closer and kissed Valerian.

Valerian kissed him back, but this morning, he had no patience. He kept the kiss short before scrambling out of bed and leaving Cooper behind as he went to the bathroom to wash up.

"What has you in such a rush?" Cooper asked from the bedroom.

"How can you ask that? Aren't you excited?"

"I am. It doesn't mean we can't stay in bed for a bit longer."

Valerian poked his head out of the bathroom. "We'll have all the time we need to stay in bed once this is done."

Cooper's smiled fondly. "I guess that's true. It's just hard to imagine that in a few hours I'll be back."

"It's still what you want?" That was the only thing Valerian needed to be sure of.

"I haven't changed my mind." Cooper sat up. "I want this. I want a life with you, and it'll be easier if I'm corporeal. I also want to be a true clan member, and that won't happen if I'm not permanently corporeal."

"That's not exactly true, but I get what you're saying. I just want this to be over with, you know? We've been thinking about this for so long that it almost feels like a dream. I don't want to dream about our future anymore, Cooper. I want our future to start today and stop being a dream."

Making Cooper corporeal wouldn't change anything in the fight against the cockatrice shifters. No one had heard from Curt since he'd run away yesterday, but Valerian had been watching the news. The journalists who'd been there when Curt had escaped had splashed the pictures and the news all over the city. From what Valerian had seen, there was a group of them camping out in front of cockatrice territory at the moment. They were trying to talk to Curt or the alpha, but as far as Valerian knew, neither of them had agreed to see them.

Valerian wasn't surprised. Curt had left with his tail between his legs, and considering what they knew about the relationship between him and the alpha, Valerian wouldn't be surprised if the man had punished Curt for what he'd done. There was no way the cockatrice alpha had agreed to have a bunch of ghosts attack the dragons. That had had to have been entirely Curt's plan, and even though Valerian barely knew the cockatrice alpha, he knew enough to be sure Curt would pay for what he'd done.

But that wasn't his problem. The only thing that mattered to him was Cooper, and he was about to become corporeal again, and permanently this time.

Valerian rushed through washing up, then dressing. He wanted to skip breakfast, but Victor had made him promise he wouldn't start anything until Gunther and Amelia arrived. Valerian had to wait for them, and he might as well get something to eat as he did so.

This morning, everyone was gathered in the dining room. They all looked as nervous as Valerian, but no one said anything. They acted as if everything was normal, and Valerian could have kissed them for that. It made it easier to breathe and relax, at least until Amelia and Gunther came in.

Then the tiny dragons in Valerian's stomach took flight again.

Amelia's smile was gentle, as always. "Are you ready?"

"I've been ready since I woke up this morning." Valerian got to his feet. "Where are we doing this?"

"We thought it would be better to do it outside, just in case," Gunther said. He smiled at Valerian, too. "I'm impressed by what you did yesterday, and damn proud, even though I'm not sure it's my place to be. You're growing into your powers."

It was true. Valerian didn't want to think about it now, because he had better things to focus on, but hearing that Gunther was proud of him still touched him. Since his parents had died, no one had been proud of him.

The group made their way outside. They found a stone bench that was far enough away from the house that no one would bother them, and Gunther and Amelia had Valerian sit down. Valerian almost protested, but then he decided it might not be a bad idea. He hadn't channeled very much power from Leo yesterday, but that would change today, and he didn't know how his body would react. It was better for him to be sitting.

"All right," Amelia said, looking at the group. "I need everyone to take a few steps back. I'm not asking you to leave, because I know it would be useless, but we need to give Valerian space, and if he does want to be alone, you'll have to go."

"I'm fine with them staying," Valerian said. The dragons present today had all volunteered to give him their magic, and he wasn't about to kick the psychics out. Everyone here cared about Cooper and wanted this for him.

Amelia nodded. "I want anyone who volunteered to step forward," she ordered. She didn't look like the gentle older woman she was anymore. She'd taken charge, and the teacher in her shone through.

Jerome, Marcel, Tim, and Leo stepped forward as one.

Amelia rolled her eyes and chuckled, then gestured at Leo, who was inching closer and closer as if he wanted to be sure he'd be the first one chosen.

"I get it," Amelia told the others. "Leo, you can sit next to him. If he needs more power, I want another dragon to be ready to give it to him. He won't be able to stop touching Cooper, which means the second dragon will have to touch him. Maybe on the neck? I don't think it matters where you touch him, just that you do it carefully so as to not startle him out of what he's doing."

Jerome's brother stepped forward, but Jerome grabbed his shoulder and pulled him back. He then walked around Valerian and touched the back of his neck, and Valerian sucked in a breath.

He didn't know what to think of Jerome, and now wasn't the moment to have doubts about this. Jerome had volunteered. He wouldn't have if he didn't want Valerian to take his magic.

"Cooper, move in front of Valerian. You can hold hands, but I think it would be better if you were to touch Valerian in a second spot. It's just in case he faints or lets go."

"He might faint?" Cooper asked, but Amelia couldn't see or hear him.

"I'll be fine," Valerian promised.

Cooper stared at him for a moment before nodding and sitting in front of him. He put one of his hands on Valerian's knee, and Valerian linked their fingers together. With the other hand, Cooper wrapped it around Valerian's ankle. They were skin to skin, and it gave Valerian a shiver of pleasure, but that would come later. Right now, he needed to be focused on making Cooper corporeal permanently.

Leo held out his hand, and Valerian took it before looking at Amelia.

She nodded. "I honestly don't know how you did it. Just

do what feels right and what you did yesterday."

Valerian decided to follow his instincts. They'd worked until now, and he didn't see why that should change. He closed his eyes and followed the crackle of power he could feel on his skin. It led him right to Leo, and Valerian just had to reach out with his ability for Leo's dragon magic to react to him.

It was almost as if it was welcoming him. It felt strong and warm, and Valerian was stunned to realize he couldn't feel the end of it. He didn't want to take too much because he had no idea what might happen to Leo if he did, but there was another warm hand on the back of his neck. He didn't recognize this magic because he'd never felt it before, but he knew it belonged to Jerome and gently pulled from it. That way he could be sure he wouldn't take too much from either of them, or at least, he hoped so. If he felt it was too much, though, he just had to say the word, and another dragon would take their place.

He could do this. They all could.

Valerian sucked in a breath and pulled harder.

For a moment, it felt like nothing was happening. Cooper didn't feel any different, but he supposed he was more focused on Valerian and how he was doing. Cooper would never forgive himself if something happened to Valerian or either of the two dragons helping them through this. They'd volunteered and knew it might spell trouble for them, but it hadn't been enough for them to change their mind. Cooper would always owe them, and he'd find a way to thank them.

To Cooper's surprise, Gunther stepped forward. He pressed his fingertips against the skin of Valerian's throat and closed his eyes, and Cooper wondered what he was doing. He wasn't worried. Gunther was a friend, and he'd never do anything to hurt either Valerian or Cooper. It was probably a good thing to have him do whatever he was doing at the moment. He had more experience than Valerian, and he'd be able to tell if something was wrong.

Cooper sucked in a breath when the power reached him. He'd felt it yesterday, too, but it had only lasted for a few moments. This time, it went on and on until Cooper felt like his skin was crawling and his body was about to explode. He knew that wouldn't happen, but it was still an odd sensation he didn't know how to deal with.

He knew the moment he became visible. The group behind them started whispering to each other, but Cooper didn't pay too much attention. He was focused on the power flowing through him, and he could feel himself changing.

Being a ghost was odd. He couldn't feel anything physically unless he was touching Valerian. It was almost like living in a dream, but that was no longer so. Cooper could feel the hard earth under his ass. He could feel Valerian's hair tickling his palm where he'd wrapped it around Valerian's ankle. He could feel himself breathing, even though he didn't need to in order to survive. He could hear the sound of the birds in the trees around them, the people talking behind him, and even the sounds of the cars passing by. He could feel the wind on his skin, something that startled him. He couldn't feel pain, but he could feel pleasure, although not as strongly as when he was alive. He'd made his peace with that, and it hadn't made him change his mind about this.

Nothing would.

Everything became clearer, but the power kept coming until it was almost too much. Cooper resisted the urge to snatch his hand back when it started feeling like an electric current. He had no idea how Valerian would know when to stop, but he trusted his boyfriend with his life, even though he didn't have one anymore. Valerian would never do anything to hurt him or the dragons helping him, and he needed to be sure that this would take permanently.

So Cooper sat through it, gritting his teeth when it became painful. He held on, welcoming the wave of power and magic that threatened to take over him. It pushed at him from every side, filling every single cell in his body, becoming part of him. Cooper had never felt anything like it, and he wondered if he might be about to explode like the ghost yesterday. It felt like it, and he had to resist the urge to scream.

Then everything stopped.

For a moment, Cooper felt suspended. The magic buzzed under his skin, but it no longer threatened to overwhelm him. It was almost as if it was settling in, filling Cooper's body and animating it. Cooper was afraid to open his eyes, but he needed to see Valerian and make sure he was all right.

He took a moment to assess how he was feeling. He didn't feel any different from when he'd been a ghost, yet at the same time, everything was different. He felt things more securely, like how hard the earth was under his ass or the wind on his skin. Before, they'd only been sensations that he hadn't been sure were real. He'd often wondered if he was imagining them and remembering how it felt, but now, he had no doubt that he *could* feel them. He could feel the wind.

And Valerian.

Cooper blinked his eyes open. Valerian was still on the bench, holding onto Leo and Cooper. His eyes were open now, and he was staring at Cooper with wide eyes.

For a moment, Cooper couldn't look away, and he didn't want to. In Valerian's eyes, he could see his future. He didn't know what that future would be like, but he didn't need to.

"What's happening?" Olsen asked in a loud whisper.

For a second, Cooper thought it was because he couldn't see him. His stomach dropped, and he was sure it hadn't worked.

"Why are you asking that? Can't you see what's

happening?" Donahue asked.

"I mean, I see Cooper, but why are they still sitting there like that?"

Cooper huffed out a laugh. He was afraid to let go of Valerian in case this wasn't over, but they couldn't stay like this forever. "Is it done?" he asked.

"I'm pretty sure it is, since I can see you," Gunther answered with a smile. He dropped his hand and stepped away from Valerian.

Valerian turned his attention to him. "That was you, wasn't it?"

Cooper had no idea what Gunther had done, but he could tell from Valerian's expression that he'd needed that help.

Gunther nodded. "I've never dealt with a dragon's magic, let alone two. I suspected it would be overwhelming for you, maybe even too much for you to be able to work with it. I'm more experienced, and I hoped that I could help guide the magic through you and into Cooper."

"Thank you. I don't know if I would have managed without you."

"You would have. You were born to do this, Valerian. We might not know what your other abilities are or how powerful you are, but you're a psychic mage. It's in your blood."

Jerome finally let go, then Leo. The only one still touching Valerian was Cooper, and while he was tempted to stay where he was for the rest of the day, he also had so many things to do.

He first let go of Valerian's ankle. When nothing happened, he also dropped Valerian's hand and got to his feet. He turned to face the others, and everyone was beaming. The first who stepped forward was York, who launched himself into Cooper's arms. Cooper caught him easily like he had when York was a child. He hauled his brother into his arms and twirled him around, both of them laughing like idiots.

Cooper couldn't remember the last time he'd been so happy. It had worked. He was hugging his brother without touching Valerian, and he could do it anytime he wanted.

"How can we be sure it's permanent?" Valerian asked.

Cooper set his brother down and turned. He wondered the same thing but doubted anyone could answer Valerian's question. Amelia had been clear that she'd never seen this happen and had only heard about it. It was rare, so there were no certainties.

"We can't be," Amelia said gently. "I'm not even sure that the few cases I heard of involved dragon magic. How did you decide how much of it Cooper needed?"

"I didn't. I let the magic do it."

"I'm pretty sure that's not what happened. You might not have made a conscious decision, but your ability did. I suppose that knowing how much power you need is part of it, but we can experiment more later. If it's what you want, of course. I won't presume you still want to learn with me now that you have what you wanted the most."

"I do want to learn." Valerian hesitated. "But maybe we can start later?"

Amelia laughed. "I would never dream of asking you to start now. Go be with your man. Both of you deserve it."

Cooper wasn't sure he'd ever done anything that meant he deserved to have a second chance and a man like Valerian, but he wasn't about to argue. He wanted both this life and his psychic mage, and he had them.

He looked around. York was still close by, with his fingers twisted into Cooper's t-shirt. Everyone had gathered around them, and they all looked happy. Cooper hadn't understood why before, but now, he realized it was because they considered him a friend and a family member as much as he considered them the same.

That was why the clan was strong. They worked together,

lived together, and would do anything for any other clan member. Elijah didn't lead with fear, and everyone respected him. That was what made the dragons better than the cockatrices, and it was why they'd eventually win this war they hadn't started.

# Chapter Fourteen

"The man was found at the edge of cockatrice territory, but the alpha declared he wasn't a clan member. Please contact this phone number if you have any information about him."

Valerian stared at the screen. He had a hard time making sense of what he'd just seen, so much so that he wondered if he'd imagined it. He wouldn't have been surprised. After all, there was almost nothing he wanted more than to have Curt disappear from the surface of the earth.

And now, he had.

Well, technically, he was still around, at least for now. But he was dead, which meant he'd never hurt Valerian again. Valerian had a hard time believing it, but the proof was right in front of him. The anchorman was still talking about who to contact if anyone had any information about the body that had been found close to cockatrice territory. Valerian did have information, but he knew better than to call. It wouldn't help, and he didn't want to make things worse with the cockatrices. Besides, even if it made him a bad person, he didn't care that Curt was dead.

Or that the anchorman had said that Curt had been torn apart by claws.

The anchorman had wondered if the dragons were at fault, but Valerian knew that wasn't so. No dragon would have killed Curt, especially not without Elijah's authorization. This had to be the cockatrices, and while the people on TV might not understand why they'd kill one of their own, Valerian did.

Curt had gone against his alpha's orders. It didn't matter that they were cousins. The alpha had let it go until he couldn't anymore, and then he'd killed Curt. It had happened after the ghost attack, which seemed to have been the straw that broke the camel's back.

Or, in this case, Curt's back.

Valerian pressed his lips together. He wasn't about to laugh over someone's death, even if he despised that someone. Curt didn't deserve pity, but he also didn't deserve for Valerian to continue thinking about him. He was gone. Hopefully, it meant the cockatrices would stop attacking the dragons, but Valerian would withhold judgment until they saw what happened next.

He picked up his phone from the coffee table and bit his lower lip. The living room was empty except for him, which was odd. With so many people living in the house, there always seemed to be someone around. It had taken some time to get used to that, but Valerian didn't mind. He cherished the moments of quietness, but he also loved when people surrounded him, maybe because he'd been on his own for so long. He'd never have to be alone anymore, and it was worth the house being a bit noisy sometimes.

Even Cooper wasn't here. He'd told Valerian he had something to do with his brother, had kissed him, and had vanished. He was in the house somewhere, so Valerian wasn't worried. He was pretty sure Cooper would find him when he heard about this, and Valerian had a phone call to make before he did.

He wasn't trying to hide the fact that he was calling Terrence. Cooper knew Valerian had Terrence's number, just like he was aware that Terrence had been the only one who'd been nice to him when he was a prisoner. Curt had been behind the kidnapping and all of that, but Valerian held the cockatrice shifters responsible, too. They'd given Curt a place to hide and to keep Valerian. Valerian would have been free long before the dragons came for him if they hadn't.

He didn't know what Terrence would say. Valerian wanted to know what had happened, but he also wanted to try to convince Terrence to leave the cockatrices. He still didn't know what kept Terrence there and didn't think he'd ever find out. Unless Terrence told him, there was no way for him to. It probably didn't have anything to do with Curt, which meant that Curt's death wouldn't change anything in Terrence's life.

But Valerian needed to be sure Terrence was safe.

A lot of people wouldn't have understood, and sometimes, Valerian wasn't sure he did, even though he was the one who felt this way. Terrence was a cockatrice shifter, and even though he hadn't hurt Valerian, he'd kept him prisoner.

Until he hadn't. He let Valerian go, even though he'd known he'd pay for it. Valerian had never blamed him for not letting him go free sooner than he had, and he never would. Terrence had to survive, so he'd kept Valerian locked up in that bedroom. Valerian had done many things he normally wouldn't do to survive when he'd been on the streets on his own, running from the coven, so he knew the position Terrence was in.

He found Terrence's number in his phone and hit the call button. He wasn't sure Terrence would answer, but if he didn't, there was nothing Valerian would be able to do. As it was, he wasn't sure there was anything he could do anyway.

But he had to try.

"Hello?" a voice asked.

Valerian sucked in a breath. "Terrence?"

"Yeah. Who is this?"

"Valerian."

There was a moment of silence. Valerian wondered if Terrence was about to hang up, and he waited for it to happen.

The silence was heavy, and he didn't dare break it.

"What do you want?" Terrence eventually asked.

There was no anger in his tone, just a deep weariness that Valerian wanted to soothe. He didn't have feelings for Terrence beyond friendship, but friendship was enough for Valerian to be worried. "How are you?"

"You didn't call me to know how I am, so get to the point. I don't have much time, and I don't have to tell you what will happen if someone realizes who I'm talking to."

Valerian was hurt, but once again, he understood. "I wanted to ask about Curt."

Terrence snorted. "You saw that, huh?"

"The entire city saw it." And it wasn't the first time the entire city saw Curt.

While running away from dragon territory, he'd been filmed, and people had recognized him from that mess with the chief of police's brother earlier. They were starting to understand that Curt had been at the center of what had been happening in the city for a while, and they were angry. That was probably why Curt had died, although Valerian suspected he'd never find out the entire truth.

"What do you want to know?" Terrence asked.

"It wasn't a dragon. Does that mean it was a cockatrice?"

"What do you think? You know what he did."

"I also know he kidnapped and hurt me, yet the alpha didn't do anything."

"Because he doesn't care about you. He cares about his power and territory and what will happen if people decide he and Curt were working together. He's unwilling to put the clan at risk and, even more importantly, himself."

"So he got rid of the problem."

"You can say that. Yes, he gave the order, although, as far as I know, he's not the one who did it. Is that all you needed to know?"

"What can I say to convince you to leave?"

"Nothing."

"There has to be something. I understand there's a reason you can't leave, but you have to realize something bad is going to happen if you don't."

"I'm not an idiot. I know what will happen if I don't leave, and that's why I'm here. If you don't have anything else to say, I need to go."

"Wait." Valerian wasn't sure what to say, but he needed Terrence to know he was here if he needed anything. He wouldn't be surprised if Terrence had a hard time believing it, but it didn't mean he wouldn't offer. "You saved my life. It's clear there's nothing I can do to save yours, and I don't know if you need me to try, but whatever happens, remember you can always call me."

"Why would you do that? I kept you prisoner and didn't do anything when they hurt you."

"Because you *couldn't* do anything. I've never blamed you for that, Terrence, and I'm not going to start now. I just want you to know that there's more out there than the cockatrice clan. I don't know what keeps you there, but it's clear it's important. You shoulder everything on your own, but you don't have to."

"And who will help me?"

He sounded bitter, and it hurt to hear. "I will, and I'm not the only one. I know you don't have a reason to trust me, especially since I'm with the dragons now, but you're not alone, Terrence. Whenever you reach your breaking point, call me. I'll do whatever I can to make sure you get out of cockatrice territory alive."

Hopefully, that would be enough, but Valerian was afraid of what would happen if it wasn't.

Cooper could tell the conversation wasn't going well, even from the hallway. He hadn't wanted to interrupt, especially after he'd realized who Valerian was talking to, but he'd known not to go too far. Valerian would need his support once the call was over, and Cooper would be happy to provide it.

He wasn't like Valerian. He didn't feel like they owed anything to Terrence, even though he'd let Valerian go. He should have done so a lot sooner, and while Cooper understood he had a good reason not to and to stay with the cockatrices, he didn't know that reason. Even though it was important, he couldn't understand why Terrence was doing this, so in his eyes, Terrence was just another person who'd hurt Valerian.

But Valerian felt differently, and Cooper couldn't ignore that. How could he, when the pain Valerian felt for Terrence was so obvious in his voice? Besides, while Cooper didn't have a relationship with Terrence since Terrence had never been able to see him, he did know the man, probably better than Valerian. He'd spent a lot of time following him around the house, trying to find a way for Valerian to get free. He hadn't found anything, but he'd seen Terrence cry several times. He'd seen how Terrence tortured himself over what he was doing to Valerian, even though he hadn't done anything to stop it from happening. Whatever the cockatrice alpha had on Terrence, it had to be extremely important for him. He'd been willing to keep Valerian prisoner to protect it, and Cooper couldn't blame him for that. He'd do pretty much anything to keep Valerian safe, after all.

Cooper realized that Valerian had been silent for a while now. His conversation was probably over, so Cooper walked into the living room. He wasn't surprised to find Valerian sitting on the couch, staring at the phone in his hand even though the TV was on. Valerian didn't even realize Cooper was there initially. He was lost in his thoughts, and Cooper didn't want to startle him, so he moved slowly toward him.

"You've heard the news," he said once he reached his boyfriend.

Valerian blinked. "About Curt?"

"Yeah." Cooper had been with York, but he'd seen the news on his phone. Authorities were asking for people who knew anything about Curt to step forward, and while Cooper doubted anyone would, at least Curt was dead. They'd never have to worry about him ever again.

That didn't mean they didn't have to worry about anything. The cockatrices had calmed down, but now, they'd dealt with their biggest problem. Who was to say they wouldn't come at the dragons again? The problems between dragons and cockatrices went beyond Curt, and they wouldn't stop just because he was dead.

Cooper sat on the couch and wrapped an arm around Valerian's shoulders. Valerian leaned against him, naturally taking his place pressed against Cooper's chest.

"I called Terrence," he said.

"I heard the end of the conversation. He's still refusing to leave?"

"Yeah. He did confirm that the alpha was the one behind Curt's death, though. I guess he had enough of Curt doing things on his own."

Especially since the things Curt did were stupid. The ghost attack especially had been a disaster, and Curt had been filmed running away from the house. He wouldn't have been able to explain it, which was probably one of the reasons the alpha had killed him.

So much for family.

"If he ever reaches out, we'll help him," Cooper tried to comfort Valerian.

Valerian sighed. "I know. I just worry that he'll never have the opportunity to reach out."

Cooper wondered about that, too, but there was nothing either of them could do. If Terrence was ever to leave the cockatrices, he'd have to be the one to take that step. Cooper and Valerian would help him as much as he needed once he had, but until then, they were powerless.

No matter how little they liked it.

# Epilogue

Dinner was lively, but then, it always was. Not every clan member came to every dinner, but there were always a lot of people, and Valerian had come to love it. He'd never feel alone again. He'd never *be* alone again, even when he wished he could be. That was the price to pay to live with a dragon clan, though, and he gladly did.

"I just don't get it," Olsen said from the other side of the table. "He was a dick, but they were family, right? I'd never kill any of my brothers." He paused and cocked his head. "Except maybe Donahue. Him, I could do without."

"Hey!" Donahue said from his seat a few chairs down from Olsen. "I'm your favorite, and you know it."

"Do I? I'm pretty sure my favorite is Victor. He's so quiet and nice."

"I can be nice, too," Donahue insisted.

"I'll believe it when I see it."

Valerian hid his smile behind his glass of water. Yes, meals especially were hard on his ears and his peace, but he wouldn't have it any other way.

"Would you have one of your clan members killed?" Olsen asked Elijah.

Everyone around the table went quiet. They knew the answer, but they were still curious.

Elijah put down his fork. "No, I wouldn't kill one of my clan members. I do understand why the cockatrice alpha did, though."

"But they were cousins. Would you kill a member of your

family?"

"The clan is my family. Dragons and cockatrices have never gotten along, and there's a reason for that. We don't see life the same way and we deal with things differently. Curt was a problem for the cockatrice clan, and when he didn't stop being one, they took care of him the only way they could think of. Dead, he can't do anything to hurt the clan."

"He also can't breathe or do anything else," Olsen muttered. "So the clan is really that important to the alpha."

"Our clans are everything to us. They're family, but also our people, and we have to protect all of that. I don't care much about the house or clan territory, but I'd do pretty much anything to protect the clan members."

Valerian doubted the cockatrice alpha had the same explanation for what he'd done. Sure, he'd killed Curt because he was a danger to the clan, but more importantly, he was a danger to the cockatrice alpha. People had started to talk about him being unable to control his people, and Curt had brought a lot of attention to the cockatrices. Considering what happened in their territory—people being kidnapped and locked up, as Valerian knew—Valerian wasn't surprised the alpha hadn't wanted people to look into him and his clan.

"Do you think it's over?" Victor asked more quietly.

Elijah didn't hesitate. "The fight between the cockatrices and the dragons will never end. For some reason, the cockatrices have always held a grudge against us, and I suspect that's why they allowed Curt to do much of what he did. They thought it would help them against us, but unfortunately for them, they were wrong."

And Curt had paid the price.

Valerian agreed, though. The cockatrices had thought that Curt could give them what they wanted, which was a win against the dragons. They'd gotten rid of him when they realized he couldn't. If that didn't expose the fact that they'd do pretty much anything to win against the dragons, Valerian wasn't sure what did.

So they'd attack again. For the moment, they were quiet, but it wouldn't last forever. Valerian didn't know what he'd do when it finally happened, but he reminded himself that he wouldn't face this on his own. He and the clan would face this as a family, and it was what they were. It didn't matter how weird it felt or that Valerian didn't know how to behave most of the time.

The clan was his future, and he'd fight to keep it intact.


Cooper shoveled another forkful of mac & cheese into his mouth and chewed. He was still weirded out by what his body could and couldn't do, but he loved the fact that he could eat again. He'd been stuffing his face since he'd become corporeal, and he wasn't planning to stop anytime soon.

Especially since he'd found out he couldn't put on weight.

It was weird. He was still dead, yet, he had a body. He and Valerian had been experimenting, trying to find out what Cooper could do and what he should avoid. Cooper could eat, something he'd been doing with enthusiasm since he'd realized it. He didn't have normal body processes anymore. He didn't need to use the bathroom, and when he got hurt, he didn't bleed. It meant he didn't have to eat or sleep, but he did both and loved it. He might not be human anymore, but he could behave like a human and be part of the life the people around him lived. That was all he'd wanted and what he'd obtained. It didn't matter that it was weird or that sometimes, he wondered if it had been the right choice.

He knew it was.

Cooper suspected that he would never age. How could he, since he was dead? That meant he'd have to watch the people he cared the most about grow old, and he wasn't looking forward to it, but he'd deal with it when it happened. And eventually, when York and Valerian passed away, Cooper would go with them. He had no interest in staying behind if he wasn't with the people he loved. He didn't know how they'd do it yet, but they had a lifetime to find out, which was all Cooper had wanted.

Not that his new life would be easy. The cockatrices weren't done with the dragons, and no one knew what their next step would be. They'd find out, eventually, and Cooper doubted they'd like it. Like they had with Curt, though, they'd fight back. It was what being a clan member meant, and he was glad he had this opportunity. He would never have thought it possible before he died, and maybe it wouldn't have been.

But now, he had a clan, and even with the enemy looming close, he knew they'd eventually win. After all, they had many psychics and a mage on their side, and of course, there was Valerian.

Cooper's psychic of all trades.

# About the Author

Catherine is the creator of several series, most of them paranormal, including the Whitedell Pride Series and the Gillham Pack Series. While she graduated in translation, she decided to go the writer's way because it was more fun to create her own stories and characters.

She's been living in Italy for more than twenty years, but she's a daughter of the North—Belgium to be precise—and she misses it so much that she's already planning to move back.

She loves pizza—probably too much—her son, her pets, and of course, books. She sneaks some reading time into her schedule every time she has five minutes free from writing, demands from her various pets and son, and lastly, housework.

Connect with her:

lievens.catherine@gmail.com
BookBub: https://www.bookbub.com/authors/catherine-lievens
Website: https://authorcatherinelievens.com/
Facebook: https://www.facebook.com/catherine.lievens.9
Facebook Group: https://www.facebook.com/groups/411788002341528/
Twitter: https://twitter.com/authorCLievens
Newsletter: http://eepurl.com/c-uvKn